Welco ters' trilogy
LOVE

An aw writes
roman won't
forget, ion.

Meet Annabelle, Gerard and Diana. Annabelle and
Gerard are private investigators, Diana their hardworking
assistant. Each of them is about to face a rather different
assignment—falling in love!

Their mission is marriage!

Books in this series are:

UNDERCOVER FIANCÉE
Annabelle has only ever loved one man—her ex-fiancé
Rand Dumbarton. Now the tycoon is back in her life and
he wants to hire Annabelle. But does he want her for
business or as his bride?

UNDERCOVER BACHELOR
Gerard Roch has given up on love since the death of his
first wife. Going undercover to catch a spy, he doesn't
expect to find himself attracted to an eighteen-year-old
temptress. But is Whitney Lawrence really what she
seems...?

UNDERCOVER BABY
Diana Rawlins turned up at the hospital with amnesia
and a baby in her arms! She doesn't remember how
either of them happened. Her husband, Cal, is
determined to get to the bottom of the mystery—
especially as that seems to be the only way he can save
his marriage!

Rebecca Winters, an American writer and mother of four, is a graduate of the University of Utah. She has won the National Readers' Choice Award, the *Romantic Times* Reviewer's Choice award and been named Utah Writer of the Year.

UNDERCOVER BACHELOR

BY
REBECCA WINTERS

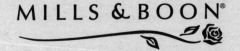

MILLS & BOON®

First published in Great Britain 1999
Harlequin Mills & Boon Limited,
Eton House, 18-24 Paradise Road, Richmond, Surrey TW9 1SR

© Rebecca Winters 1999

ISBN 0 263 81751 2

Set in Times Roman 10½ on 12¼ pt.
02-9908-45992 C1

Printed and bound in Spain
by Litografia Rosés, S.A., Barcelona

CHAPTER ONE

"ARE you saying it was a man on your tour of France last year who made you pregnant?"

Whitney Lawrence tried to hide her shock in front of her half sister Christine who was trying to keep Greg, her little five-month-old son, quiet by giving him another bottle.

They'd met for a quick lunch at a crowded downtown Salt Lake restaurant near the law firm where Whitney worked.

Up until this second, Christine had patently refused to tell the family who Greg's father was. But all along Whitney had suspected it was one of the boys on Christine's same tour bus, or a French boy she'd met in Paris or Nice. One moreover who didn't have a clue he was now the father of the adorable little baby Christine was feeding right now.

After a long interval Christine nodded. "He was wonderful to me, Whitney, and so good-looking. When he told me he loved me, I was so happy, I—I couldn't help myself."

Bile rose in Whitney's throat. "Did he force you?"

"No. It wasn't like that. Just the opposite in fact." She tossed her head back to reveal tear-stained cheeks. "When he confided to me that he was separated from his wife who'd been seeing another man for a long time, I—I didn't feel as guilty about getting close to him.

"He said their marriage had been over for ages, and the only reason he hadn't divorced her yet was because he was waiting until their four-year-old daughter was a little older and could handle it."

At that revelation Whitney's hand froze around the extra baby blanket before she pulled it from the diaper bag to give Christine. There seemed to be a slight draft where they were sitting. Greg needed a little more protection.

"Toward the end of the tour he thanked me for listening to him and admitted that he was falling in love with me. But he apologized for saying anything because he knew I was too young for him.

"I told him I loved him, too, and I kissed him to prove it. One thing led to another, and you know what happened. The day before I had to fly home we planned to shop and spend some time alone together. But he wasn't feeling well so I volunteered to pick up a toy he'd ordered ahead of time for his daughter."

"Did you end up paying for that, too?" Whitney was heartsick for her.

"No. He gave me an envelope of money. When I returned with the package, he was feeling better. We made love again, but that was the last time. He never called or wrote me after I got back to Salt Lake.

"That's when I realized I'd been used. I vowed never to tell anyone. But then I found out I was expecting Greg." Her voice broke. She lifted the baby to her shoulder to burp him.

Whitney was proud of Christine, who had turned into a wonderful mother. But it had to be an overwhelming job without a husband's support.

"Oh, honey—" she murmured compassionately. To

a naive, foolish eighteen-year-old teenager seeing the world for the first time, an attractive man's exclusive interest meant love at first sight, no matter what fairy tales he told. It all went with the territory. *And some unscrupulous male had preyed on that knowledge.*

"He didn't even mention the word protection, did he?"

The moment the question was out, her sister's pretty features hardened. Whitney knew she'd hit a nerve. "I don't want to talk about it anymore. I wish I hadn't brought it up. Promise me you won't say one word of this to Mom or Dad."

"I promise."

Whitney knew better than to press the issue. She wouldn't get anything more out of her sister. In fact it was a miracle she'd revealed this much.

Sitting back in the chair, Whitney toyed with her burrito, unable to eat it. Either a male teacher, the driver, or the tour guide was Greg's father.

The more she thought about it, the more she figured it was probably Christine's French teacher, Mr. Bowen. After taking French from him for three years, she'd talked their mom and Whitney's stepfather into letting her go on one of the student trips to France he organized twice a year. She'd been so crazy about him, she'd even nominated him for teacher of the year.

What was the saying? These kinds of situations generally happened to people you knew well?

The *fiend* was still running around loose with his students. No telling how many other willing teenage girls he'd talked into bed.

As Whitney sat there eyeing Christine and her precious baby, her attorney's mind conceived the idea to nail that lothario for seducing her young, vulnerable sister. He'd left her pregnant, alone, and would never have to pay a penny of child support.

A stolen moment of pleasure for the jerk had changed the entire course of Christine's life! He didn't care that she had a reputation to preserve. Greg, at least, deserved to be given his father's name.

If nothing else, Whitney would find out who he was and make sure he got fired to prevent him from ever using his job to exploit other female victims again.

Already she had a plan in mind to expose him. She couldn't wait to get back to the office and put things into motion.

"Tell you what, Christine. After I get home from work this evening, I'll come over to the house. You can get out with your friends, maybe go to a movie. I'll tend my cute little nephew. I love to bathe and feed him. What do you say?"

The suggestion seemed to brighten Christine's spirits. "That would be wonderful. I'm so thankful I have you and the family. I'd never make it through otherwise."

"You're not only going to make it through, you and Greg are going to have a wonderful life. *I swear it.*"

"*Comrade?* Phil said you wanted to see me."

"I'm glad you got the message, *Comrade.* Come on in and shut the door. Someone from Interpol has been anxious to reach you."

Gerard Roche sat down in the chair opposite Roman's desk. "So what's new, boss? They hound me all the time to go back and work for them again.

I always tell them I'm not interested. I like the skiing here just fine.''

Roman smiled. ''Amen to that. Besides, I've gotten used to my best PI solving the toughest cases. I refuse to lose you. If Yuri thought you were going back to Europe to work for Interpol again, I'm afraid you would have to answer to him, as well.''

The mention of Roman's elder brother Yuri brought a grin to Gerard's face. Roman and Yuri Lufka, short for Lufkilovich, denoting their Russian ancestry, were two of Gerard's best friends.

There was nothing Gerard loved more than getting out on the ski slopes with both brothers who were not only great sportsmen, but phenomenal linguists. Together they managed to slaughter Russian, German, French and a few Slavic dialects at once, much to the amusement of their friends and colleagues. Yuri and his family flew to Salt Lake from New York every month for business and pleasure.

Between all of them, plus the other PI's and Gerard's parents who resided in Alta, a mountain town thirty minutes from Salt Lake, Gerard's life was full. If he moved out of the country, the opportunities to visit the people he loved would vanish.

No way would he ever live in Europe again. The avalanche that had claimed his wife's life in Switzerland years ago had brought an end to many dreams. He had no desire to go back.

''I've just finished tying up the loose ends on the Burrow's case and am ready to take on a new one, Roman. How about a witness protection assignment in the mountains where I can trade off with one of the guys and still get in some serious rock climbing?''

"When that case arises, you'll be the first one to hear about it."

Gerard stretched his long legs out in front of him. "In other words, you've got something on the docket I'm not going to like."

Roman's gaze scrutinized him. "I'm not sure. You don't have to take it."

"Now you're intriguing me."

"Interpol has had its eye on a man suspected of being a plant for a foreign government, probably eastern Europe, but they're not sure. The name he's currently using is Donald Bowen. The man has a wife and child. They're still checking on the status of his wife.

"For the last seven years he's been posing as a French teacher at a high school here in Salt Lake. During that period, he's been part of a group of teachers taking their students to France and Switzerland in the spring, summer.

"It's believed that during these trips, he acts as a go-between for an agent selling classified American military secrets to a Middle Eastern government. Unfortunately he has eluded Interpol's best efforts.

"Though you're a civilian now, they'd like your cooperation and are willing to pay for your time to help catch him in the act. They'll supply all the backup you need. It would mean traveling to France and Switzerland in June."

Roman eyed Gerard soberly. "If the memory of your wife, Simone, still hurts too much, then forget I said anything."

"It's all right, Roman. I let go of her a long time ago. Otherwise I wouldn't have enjoyed female company since then, particularly Annabelle's—when she would let me.''

At that remark, both of them chuckled. Gerard had liked Annabelle Forrester, another PI with the firm, more than any woman since Simone.

It had been the now-very-married Annabelle who, when she'd first come to work for Roman, had found out Gerard had been christened Eric-Gerard because of his German father and French-Swiss mother. At that point in time Annabelle had insisted that everyone stop calling him Eric and start referring to him as Gerard. She thought his French name sounded much more exciting and romantic.

Soon Diana, Roman's private secretary, was calling him Gerard. What started out as a joke became the status quo as one PI after another followed suit. Roman finally made the decision that everyone call him Gerard so there would be no more confusion.

Not only did Gerard find Annabelle highly amusing, she was smart and adorable, but a little too elusive at times. Or maybe he used that as an excuse because he hadn't been ready to make another commitment that could end in tragedy.

All the same, it was a bitter pill to swallow when Rand Dunbarton, Annabelle's ex-fiancé and client, had moved to Salt Lake from Phoenix and had ended up marrying her. He was a lucky man and Gerard envied him.

''My problem is, I haven't been to Switzerland since the accident.''

Roman folded his arms. ''The trip will definitely stir up memories. For that reason I'm not pushing you on this one.''

Gerard was pensive. "Maybe it's time to face my ghosts."

"Only if you want to. Interpol will probably pay any fee you ask within reason to obtain your help. I'm told they've looked at other private detectives in the area, but naturally you're their first choice because of your excellent work record with them, not to mention your fluency in French and German and your knowledge of Europe."

"Spare me the litany," Gerard interjected. "Even I have to admit I'm a natural for the assignment."

"You are. No one else on this staff or any other would begin to qualify."

"Tell me what my cover would be."

"A divorced high school French teacher."

"You must be joking. A sort of glorified *Kindergarten Cop*?"

That drew another chuckle out of Roman. "According to Brittany, and I quote, you bear 'a superficial resemblence to Arnold Schwarzenegger, only you're much better looking.'"

Gerard's brows lifted. "Your beautiful wife said that about me?"

"She did."

"Were you jealous?"

Again, the two men shared a quiet laugh.

"Interpol has decided that only a teacher on the same tour can monitor this guy's movements day and night without suspicion. He uses a local company called STI, Student Teacher International.

"This agency flies a busload of Utah teachers and students to Paris where they connect with their European tour guide. Your job would be to help chaperone the students and get chummy with Bowen at the same time."

Gerard sat forward. "I've gone undercover in hundreds of ways, but I don't like the idea of using kids to get the job done."

"Your target has no such compunction. That's one of the reasons why Interpol wants to get the goods on this traitor so they can put him away permanently."

"When is all this going to happen?"

"The tour leaves June fifth from Salt Lake International Airport on a special charter flying to Paris. You'll be gone ten days for a tour of Eastern France and Switzerland."

"I assume Interpol has done all the paperwork?"

"Take a look." Roman pulled a passport out of an envelope sitting on the desk and handed it to him.

They stared at each other. "I was their *first* choice? *Hell,* I was their *only* choice!"

"That's because you're the best," his friend said with convincing sincerity.

Gerard didn't have to peer inside to know his own picture had been put there along with all the false identification. Deciding to get this over with, he opened the cover and saw his image staring up at him. Hank Smith, age thirty-eight, male from Utah, issued by the San Francisco office.

"*Hank Smith?* I wonder which idiot came up with that one?"

"Hank suits you, and there are more Smiths living in Utah than any other name. It all makes sense." Roman winked. "According to the rest of the documentation, you're a French teacher from St. George, Utah, who decided too late to sign up your own students. You're willing to take any other teacher's over-flow and will pay full price for the opportunity so you'll know how to organize for next year's tour.''

"High school kids, huh?"

Roman flashed him a wry smile. "From what I understand, foreign language students are the better, more well-behaved bunch, but I have no doubts it will still be a challenge."

"That's one way of putting it," Gerard bit out.

"There's a meeting next Wednesday night at the Salt Lake Library downtown where the students and teachers get acquainted. Then there will be a final meeting a week from Wednesday night at the same place to go over last-minute instructions and give out tickets. It's all in here." Roman handed him the thick envelope.

"That next meeting is only four days from now."

"I won't assign you anything else to give you time to prepare."

"I don't know, Roman."

"If you can't make a decision yet, then don't. I'm still giving you the time off. Go rock climbing for a couple of days. That'll clear your head. Call me when you know what you want to do. I'll deliver the message to Interpol, whatever it is."

"Thanks, Roman. I'll think about it."

"Next, please. Your name?"

"Whitney Lawrence. Union High School."

"I don't see... Oh, yes. You're one of the students wishing to travel with Mr. Bowen, but he's full. We've assigned you to Mr. Smith's group."

"But I have to be with Mr. Bowen! One of my

friends was on tour with him last year and loved him.
That's the only reason I signed up.''

*That was the whole point of the situation in which
Whitney had purposely placed herself.*

"Everyone wants to be with Mr. Bowen because
he's such a popular French teacher. But you signed up
too late. His students were already organizing for the
trip last fall. Fortunately, Mr. Smith has room. He's a
fine French teacher, too. Don't worry,'' she said when
Whitney made a long face. "You'll all be on the same
bus together.''

"Oh. Okay,'' Whitney sighed out loud dramatically,
hoping her reaction was that of a typical teen.
Inwardly, she felt instant relief at the news.

"Everyone is meeting in the room at the far end of
the hall. Here's your name tag. Put it on so you'll be
recognized.''

"Thanks.''

Whitney took the tag and pinned it to the vest she
wore over her short-sleeved blouse. Wearing sneakers,
white socks and thigh-length cutoffs, her outfit resem-
bled those of every teenage girl lined up in the hall of
the library.

With her hair falling to her shoulders, the top portion caught near the crown with a clip, her hairdo
blended with all the other hairdos which were more or
less the same. Minus any makeup and blessed with her
mother's young skin, Whitney prayed she looked the
eighteen years she was purporting to be. Only her
passport would betray her, and she wasn't letting it
out of her possession for any reason.

She'd deliberately waited until this last meeting to
show up, wanting to keep as low a profile as possible.

Everyone at the Sharp and Rowe law firm would be shocked to see their newest attorney, who had just passed the Utah bar, passing herself off as a teenager. But no one could know she was on a mission to expose the man responsible for getting Christine pregnant.

Of course it was possible her plan wouldn't work. But better she use the vacation time coming to her since studying for the bar to try and track down the culprit, than stay at home brooding over her sister's pain.

It wasn't fair that a man got off scot-free in a situation like this. It happened all the time, all over the world, but that didn't make it right. If she could carry out this tricky scheme for her sister's sake and discover his identity, it was possible the father might suffer an attack of conscience and help pay child support. If nothing else, Whitney felt it would have been well worth the subterfuge for that much satisfaction.

Her family believed she was taking off to Mexico with a couple of friends she'd met while going to law school. If she couldn't find Greg's biological father, Whitney didn't want to tell her family what she'd done. But if she was successful, that would be a different story.

Therefore, instead of sending the occasional postcard home which would give away a European location, she intended to make a couple of phone calls to the family so they wouldn't become suspicious or worry. Christine had promised to go by Whitney's apartment every day to check the mail and water the plants.

John Warren, a fellow attorney who'd been one of

her study partners through college and had passed the bar at the same time as she had, was the only person who knew her plans.

When he heard what had happened to Christine and listened to Whitney's idea to catch the teacher responsible, John applauded her plan, but he didn't buy the teacher theory. Rather he tended to believe that the tour guide or the driver had been the one to charm her sister into bed.

To Whitney's surprise, she discovered that John didn't like or trust European men. Apparently he'd had a cousin who'd gone to Europe on a music tour and had gotten involved with some Austrian tour guide in Vienna who had only been playing around. It ruined her life for a long time.

Happy to help Whitney even the score, he volunteered to subpoena STI's records on some pretext to obtain the names of the tour guide and bus driver on Christine's tour.

Armed with the necessary information, Whitney had been able to request a tour that included the same teacher, driver and tour guide who'd been on Christine's trip. It was leaving June fifth.

That day was almost here, Whitney mused as she stepped inside the doors of one of the library meeting rooms. At a glance it seemed forty or so students were standing in separate lines before tables placed around the room.

Pennants in different colors with teachers' names had been mounted alphabetically on the walls above each table: Ms. Ashton, Mr. LeCheminant, Mrs. Donetti, Mr. Hart, Mr. Grimshaw, Mr. Smith, Mr. Bowen and Mr. Sorenson.

The teachers hadn't come in yet.

Whitney was probably the last student to arrive and took her place behind a couple of boys talking animatedly about how much spending money they were taking with them.

On their tags she saw that the one named Jeff from Ephriam High was her height, five feet nine. The other named Roger from Dixie High was maybe an inch taller with a more robust build. Both had dark brown hair and they were cute.

As soon as they saw her, they stopped talking and just stared.

"Hi, guys."

"Hi!" they said in unison, their faces breaking into huge smiles. "Are you one of Mr. Smith's students?"

"No. I had planned to go with Mr. Bowen's group, but I signed up too late, so they put me with Mr. Smith."

"The same thing happened to us." They spoke in unison again and the three of them laughed congenially.

"Where's Union High?"

"Up in Park Valley. Box Elder County."

"How many years of French have you taken, Whitney?" Jeff asked.

"Two." Junior high seemed an awfully long time ago. "How about you?"

"Six years for me."

"Me, too," Roger chimed in.

"Wow. You guys must be good."

"Of course." Jeff grinned.

Roger said, "My French teacher goes over to France every summer, but she doesn't want to take kids around, so she called STI and they assigned me to Mr. Smith who teaches in St. George.''

''We thought we were the only ones going with him. Looks like we thought wrong.'' They grinned as if they'd just won the lottery.

Had she ever been this young and immature?

''I was afraid there would only be girls on the tour,'' Whitney murmured, deciding she'd better start doing her share of flirting. That's what teenage girls did all the time. *Shamelessly.* ''I'm glad I was wrong.''

''This is already turning out to be a great trip and we haven't even left yet,'' Roger enthused.

''Since the three of us will have rooms by each other and eat meals together, we can help you out with your French in case you have any problems.''

''Thanks, Jeff. I might have to take you up on that.'' She smiled into his eyes.

''No problem.''

''Have you guys met Mr. Smith yet?''

''Yeah. He's awesome.''

''I like him a lot better than my own teacher,'' Roger stated.

''I'm glad you said that because my teacher in Park Valley was an old battle-ax.''

''Battle-ax?'' Jeff laughed.

Uh-oh. Whitney realized that wasn't a word today's teenager used. ''That's what my dad called her when he had her for French.''

Before her father had died of a stroke and her mother had married Christine's father, Whitney adored listening to her dad's amusing tales about his school days. She would always miss him.

"Your French teacher used to teach your dad?" Roger demanded incredulously.

That part was a lie, but Whitney nodded without any compunction. The guys thought it was hilarious and both of them laughed. While she waited for them to calm down, the teachers filed in the room toward the tables, carrying stacks of manila-colored packets.

There were eight adults, but Whitney saw only one person—a man with dark blond, fairly short-cropped hair and a bronzed complexion who had to be at least six feet three inches of hard muscle.

He was dressed in a silky-looking gray suit with a charcoal-colored shirt open at the neck, very sophisticated and cosmopolitan. Sporting an expensive-looking gold watch, he didn't look like any teacher she'd ever had.

Strong and fit, he moved with unconscious male grace, like someone who was used to being in the out-of-doors rather than a schoolroom. Probably closer to forty than thirty, his bone structure was reminiscent of western European ancestry.

The square jaw with its hint of five o'clock shadow and his straight nose kept him from being handsome in the accepted sense, yet his features made him much more interesting. He exuded confidence and an unconscious masculine appeal that called to everything feminine in her.

Whitney couldn't remember the last time a man had made this kind of an impact on her. No woman young or old could remain immune to such unquestioned masculinity.

If he affects you this way, can you imagine how devastating his sex appeal had been to Christine? A seventeen-going-on-eighteen-year-old girl alone in Europe on the verge of womanhood?

Whitney's instincts had been right all along. *Christine's French teacher, Mr. Bowen, was the father of her baby! Greg's fine baby hair was the same dark blond color.*

The guys were talking again, but she couldn't hear what they were saying because a comment her sister had made at lunch that day came back to haunt her.

He's so good-looking, and we grew close on the trip. When he finally told me he loved me, I—I couldn't help myself.

In an effort to get a grip on her emotions, Whitney leaned over and retied her shoelaces. She didn't need to go on the tour for answers. The man she'd been damning to hell since learning that the liar had taken advantage of Christine, had already entered the room, looking larger than life.

"Hey, Whitney?" There was a tap on her shoulder.

"Yes, Jeff?" Expelling the breath she'd been holding, she slowly stood up and turned around to see what he wanted. Looking past the smooth faces of the two teens, she received her second shock of the evening.

A pair of light gray eyes dotted with translucent green flecks held her gaze, trapping her as surely as if she'd been physically caught in a vise of some kind.

Christine had spent three years in a French class looking into those eyes? No wonder she'd never stood a chance.

For a lightning moment the world spun out of control. Sometimes in her dreams Whitney felt herself falling. That was the sensation she was experiencing now.

"Bonsoir, Whitney. Je m'appelle Monsieur Smith. C'est un grand plaisir." His deep male voice spoke in flawless French. She felt its resonance to her bones.

CHAPTER TWO

MONSIEUR SMITH?

Whitney shook her head in confusion, feeling out of breath. "Wait a minute. *You're* not Mr. Bowen?" Her voice had a definite squeaking quality to it.

The crinkles around his startlingly beautiful eyes deepened as he broke into an apologetic smile that made her insides melt. "Not the last time I looked. I'm sorry. Every student wants to be with him. I hope you won't mind putting up with me."

She blinked, trying to make sense out of everything. She'd been so positive he was Mr. Bowen!

With the greatest effort of will, she broke eye contact with him and shifted her gaze to another male teacher standing at the next table.

According to the pennant, *he* was Mr. Bowen. *But how could he be?*

The slender man with dark eyes and hard cheekbones, probably late forties, had a pale, tired-looking face and darkish hair receding at the forehead and temples. He stood a little under six feet tall. His off-white shirt and dark trousers had no particular style.

To Whitney he epitomized the typical burnt-out teacher who was slowly being worn down by stress. She couldn't imagine why he would want to herd a bunch of kids around Europe when he already did it at home nine months out of the year.

However, there was no accounting for taste.

23

According to Christine, Mr. Bowen was dynamite in the classroom and everyone adored him, but under no circumstances could Whitney imagine him setting any girl's heart on fire. Not like…

As if a lodestone were pulling her inexorably toward its magnetic field, Whitney's gaze swerved back to the man whose mere presence had quickened her pulse.

Christine had never mentioned anything about a Mr. Smith being on her tour. But naturally, she wouldn't have. Not when she'd wanted to keep the nature of her relationship with him a secret from everyone.

A flood of heat swept through Whitney's body because the man in question had caught her practically devouring him with her eyes. It certainly wasn't the kind of stare a female student should be giving her male teacher no matter how attractive he was. Christine had probably given him the same stare!

On the other hand, he was the *teacher!* He had no business sending any young female student that frank, unmistakable look of male appreciation. His eyes had literally illuminated as they'd traveled over her.

If *that* was the way he'd looked at Christine the first time she'd ever seen him, it was no mystery why her poor sister had thought herself in love.

The man made you feel like Helen of Troy!

Putting two and two together, Whitney had the strongest suspicion she was looking at the father of Christine's baby. It all fit…the looks, the charisma. His charm…

Was he the culprit?

If so, the cad could have any female he wanted,

young or old, and *he knew it!* His conquests must be legion.

She wondered just how many unsuspecting teenage girls had become involved with him after hearing about his marital problems and his *poor* little four-year-old daughter.

How many girls had become pregnant as a result of carrying out his phony little errands and trying to comfort him in his agony?

Oh, Mr. Smith, the way you were looking at me just now tells me you're the man I'm searching for.

You play a very dangerous game, but for once you've met someone who knows the score. Before I'm through with you, you're going to be extremely sorry you picked me for your next victim.

As soon as Gerard realized he'd been staring at this feminine addition to his tour group, he recognized his mistake and shifted his gaze to the boys who were obviously enthralled by her presence.

He hoped to heaven he was wrong, but it seemed Ms. Lawrence was as aware of him as he was of her. *That was all he needed.*

How was he supposed to do a job when he had to get through the next ten days chaperoning a high school girl whose French lilac-colored eyes beckoned, whose womanly figure reminded him of a modern-day Aphrodite?

She wasn't wearing anything different than the other teenagers in the room. In fact she'd done absolutely nothing to draw attention to herself. But while she had leaned over to tie her shoes, he hadn't been able to keep his eyes off the mold of her fully curved body, or her long, shapely legs.

The truth was, in the past he'd never been attracted to tall women. He'd liked them short, dark and petite. His late wife had only stood as high as his heart.

This girl-woman, he cursed under his breath, had to be at least five-eight, five-nine. Most blondes, even ash-blondes like her, usually had fine skin coloring that required a certain amount of makeup so they wouldn't look washed out.

She didn't seem to be wearing any makeup because with that flawless young skin, she didn't need to. The faint flush which had appeared while he'd been drinking his fill of her only added natural color to her classic features. He'd never seen a female with such perfectly shaped eyebrows or lips.

Ms. Lawrence was more woman than he'd met in years. *How could she only be eighteen?*

It was common knowledge that girls her age often matured faster than boys. But somehow he hadn't expected a teenager in his group to make him think thoughts he had no business thinking by simply looking at her.

The first order of business was to get himself under control. Since Annabelle had spurned him, he hadn't actively pursued another relationship. That's what was wrong with him. If he could be this easily distracted by a girl who was young enough to be his daughter, then he'd been without a woman too long.

Maybe he'd better concentrate on returning Fran Ashton's interest since they were going to be on the same tour bus. Except that the vivacious thirty-year-old French teacher from Rosemont High had come on too strong to him at the last meeting, letting him know she was single and available. He was afraid the attraction was all on her part.

Nothing about this assignment was going the way he had planned it, and the tour hadn't even started yet.

"If you've recovered from your disappointment, Whitney, we'll go into the auditorium and watch a film which will explain about the items in your packets."

Once more their gazes met, but dark lashes partially concealed the expression in hers. "I'm sorry, Mr. Smith. I didn't mean to be rude."

"No apology necessary. You and the guys can call me Hank. I don't like standing on formality."

She'd averted her eyes, obviously still upset that she couldn't be in Mr. Bowen's group. Apparently Gerard's target was so popular with his students, even kids from around the state had heard of him.

Normally her show of disappointment wouldn't have fazed him. But there was nothing *normal* about this situation, certainly not this awareness of her or the fact that one of the teachers was suspected of passing information to a foreign government.

Much as Gerard wished Whitney Lawrence had been assigned to any other teacher than himself, he had to admit he was glad she didn't make up part of Donald Bowen's group.

The man who came off acting like he was every student's best friend, was wanted by Interpol and considered dangerous. When Gerard got the goods on him, Donald Bowen would spend the rest of his life in prison. The popular French teacher with the perfect cover to camouflage his double life was about to take his last trip to Europe.

"We'll hurry inside and save seats," Jeff volunteered. "Come on, Whitney."

For another unguarded moment Gerard received the full impact of her gaze which was appraising him in open female interest once more. It seemed that because she had caught him doing the same thing to her moments earlier, she felt she'd been given the green light to keep flirting. Her aggression shouldn't have surprised him. Teenagers these days had few inhibitions.

"You guys go ahead," he heard her say in a slightly husky voice he found far too attractive. "I need to ask Hank a couple of questions first."

Disappointment marred the boys' features as they lingered a moment longer, then walked away disgruntled.

"What's on your mind, Whitney?"

She bit softly against her lower lip where he could see her small, even white teeth. It angered him that every part of her beautiful face and body appealed to him this strongly, even the flowery scent of what could be her shampoo or perfume.

"My grandmother asked me to talk to you, but I didn't want Roger or Jeff to overhear me."

"Your grandmother?"

"Yes. She raised me. Anyway, I know this is going to sound conceited, but I can't go anywhere without guys bothering me."

Gerard could believe it. He had half a mind to call her grandmother and tell her Whitney had the kind of looks and sex appeal that shouldn't be let loose anywhere around males, particularly not in Europe. The inviting glances she'd been giving him had been duly noted. Any man without scruples, be he young or old, would consider her fair game.

"Jeff and Roger are really nice and I like them, but I had hoped there would be another girl in our group to sit with on the bus. Since there isn't, do you mind if I sit with you? Even in the movie? That way I'll have you to protect me."

He had to think fast. "I'm sure I can arrange with one of the other teachers for a female student to be your companion around Europe."

"Please don't do that!" she cried out softly. In an instant, her whole demeanor had changed. Her panic appeared real.

"Why not?"

"Because it won't work. Everyone has a friend already, and they've chosen their groups. I know what girls are like. I joined the tour too late and they won't want to include me. Besides, other girls always accuse me of trying to take away their boyfriends, even when I don't do anything! They're mean to me. It ruins e-everything."

In his gut he knew she was speaking the truth. The girls who had chosen to go to Europe would have made certain they had a friend for the trip. They most definitely wouldn't want to compete with a young woman who looked like Whitney.

"How is it you signed up to travel alone?"

Her gorgeous violet-blue eyes suddenly glistened with tears. "At the last minute, my best friend got sick and couldn't come. I live with my grandmother, and when she heard that Leslie was ill, she wanted me to cancel, but I've been waiting for this trip forever.

"I earned all the money myself and graduated with a four point average. Because of that she finally said I could go on the tour if I promised to stay by my teacher the whole time. She doesn't trust boys my age at all."

Gerard stifled a groan. This was a complication he would never have anticipated.

"A friend of my cousin's went on the trip with Mr. Bowen last year. She said he was so nice, I assumed he would take care of me. But I signed up too late to get in his group. You don't mind if I sit with you, do you, Mr. Smith? I'll be good and leave you alone. I *promise*."

The tremor in her voice brought out an unbidden, protective instinct in him he hadn't felt since long before Simone's death. It put him at odds with his initial appraisal of her and the situation. "I'll do what I can to help."

"Thanks so much," she whispered.

Right now those moist, ingenuous, lavender-blue orbs were looking at him with an expression akin to gratitude, nothing else.

Maybe he'd been wrong. Maybe he'd just imagined that she'd been sending out signals earlier. To be honest, he didn't know what to believe, but he felt it would be cruel to disregard her request when she'd worked so hard all year for this trip.

"You're welcome. Let's go next door so you won't miss hearing the instructions."

By tacit agreement they walked toward the exit. As if to prove she wouldn't be a nuisance, she didn't say another word and simply followed him from the other side of the tables. By the time they'd entered the small, semidark auditorium down the hall, the film had already started.

"Hank?" a female voice called out. He looked to his right and saw Fran Ashton who was sitting with her group. She patted the aisle seat next to her. *She'd been waiting for him.* If he sat by her now, she would assume the attraction was mutual.

Oddly enough, the clear message in her eyes irritated him even more than it had the other night. Deciding that now would be the time to let her know any interest he had in her was purely professional, he placed a hand at the back of Whitney's waist to guide her in Fran's direction.

He'd made the physical gesture without thinking, but when he felt the younger woman tremble in reaction to his touch, he realized his mistake and just as quickly removed it.

"Miss Ashton?" he murmured quietly so as not to disturb the others around them. "The auditorium is full. Do you mind if one of my students sits with you?"

The other woman looked chagrined, but she couldn't very well refuse his request. "No."

"Thank you."

To his relief Whitney brushed past him to sit down without protest. In the process, he felt the imprint of her voluptuous body. Though the contact was accidental, it ignited sensations he hadn't felt for a long time.

Dry-mouthed, he leaned over enough to murmur, "I'll see you in front of the Global Airlines' counter on Sunday morning. Six-thirty a.m. sharp."

"I can't wait. Thanks again," she said softly. Her

lips came dangerously close to his cheek where he felt her breath. Their intimate exchange quickened his pulse.

Needing some air, he left the auditorium in a few swift strides. It was his job to stay until after the film to answer his group's questions, but for the moment he craved a little privacy.

What in the hell was he was going to do with Whitney Lawrence for the next ten days? He'd all but promised her she could sit by him throughout the tour.

Roman's comment about this assignment being a challenge had turned out to be much more prophetic than either of them knew.

"Hank? Wait up!"

He heard his name called and turned around to discover Donald Bowen on his heels.

Gerard had been using ingenious ways to get to know his target better. It pleased him that the other man was the one to seek him out. Gerard was making progress.

"Hey, Don." Whether the other man liked the abbreviation or not, Gerard had decided to go with it.

Donald flashed him an easy smile. "You weren't leaving, were you?"

"No. I just wanted to get a drink. How about you?"

"Actually I've been waiting to talk to you."

"Go ahead."

"Sandy McGinnis, the woman STI sent over tonight, just informed me that you have a student named Whitney Lawrence from Union High who wanted to be assigned to my group. Apparently she was disappointed when she found out mine was full."

"I had no idea," Gerard lied, wondering where this conversation was going.

"Was it the tall blonde you brought in late? The one who sat down next to Fran?"

Like every other male on the premises, Donald Bowen had noticed Ms. Lawrence, too. "She's the one," Gerard murmured, his senses suddenly on full alert.

"When Sandy assigned her to you, she didn't realize that you only had boys in your group. She shouldn't have put a female student with you.

"My group is made up of three girls and three guys. I've already talked to Mike Sargeant, one of my boys. He'll be happy to trade. If you want, I'll talk to your student after the film and tell her she's been switched to me."

Donald Bowen never did anything without a hidden agenda. Already briefed on the man's history, Gerard couldn't figure out why Whitney's name had even come up, or how she fit into his schemes. The welfare of one student would be the last thing a foreign agent would care about.

Unless he used his female students in some capacity to help pass along information without their knowing it.

But Donald Bowen already had several of his own female students signed up for the tour. Why would he be concerned over what an unknown student from a different part of the state did or didn't do, especially when the other three girls were available?

As Gerard pondered that question, the thought briefly entered his head that Ms. Lawrence might be an accomplice coming on the scene to help him out. But he as quickly dismissed the absurd notion.

Though Whitney Lawrence could be taken for a full-grown adult, she *was* only a high school senior. When and where would she have been recruited by Donald Bowen to help him do his dirty work? It didn't make sense.

The more he thought about it, the only reason he could account for the agent's interest in Ms. Lawrence was the fact that despite her young years, she was easily one of the most attractive women Gerard had ever seen or met in his life.

If that were true for him, it would hold equally true for Donald Bowen who was a man and had eyes in his head. On or off the job, he probably went through women as a matter of course. He wouldn't worry about compromising a few willing female students in the process.

One lustful glance at Ms. Lawrence and Donald Bowen had decided to manipulate the situation to his advantage in order to assuage his desires on the tour.

To Gerard's shock, he felt a distinct distaste at the thought of the other man exploiting her for any reason.

"It's okay, Don. I'm taking her under my wing so you won't have to worry about it."

The man's smile faded. "Look, Gerard," he said in a confiding tone. "You don't understand because you haven't been a chaperone before. Her parents could cause a lot of trouble if they find out she's the only girl in the company of a bunch of guys. You can't guard them all the hours of the day and night, if you catch my drift."

Catch my drift?

That was a rather obsolete idiom a foreign agent might have learned twenty years ago, but it didn't fly with Gerard. The man's hair and bone structure put him in mind of an Eastern block type. Yuri would know his nationality at a glance. Maybe Gerard could arrange for his good friend to fly to Geneva to verify his theory.

"Her grandmother is her guardian and she'll feel fine about it when she finds out I'm taking personal charge of her."

"Then you're asking for a different kind of trouble." All pretense had fled.

"What do you mean?"

"Come on." His dark eyes narrowed. "The boys in my group have already been discussing her. One of them said she looks good enough to eat."

That was no news to Gerard.

"How do you think it's going to go over when they notice you baby-sitting her the whole time? It might look innocent to you, but that's how gossip starts."

The man was trying intimidation tactics on him. For some reason, it really upset him that Gerard wouldn't play ball where Whitney Lawrence was concerned.

"To be honest, I'm more worried about Fran Ashton," Gerard commented, pretending to misunderstand. He lowered his voice in the same confiding manner as Donald. "She's been sending out signals since last week. But nice as she is, I'm involved with someone else. Chaperoning Ms. Lawrence on the tour is going to take care of a potential problem for me. You know how it is when the attraction is only one-sided."

The other man pondered Gerard's explanation, then

shrugged in a fashion untypical of an American, as if he'd suddenly realized he'd been showing his hand too strongly.

"It happens, *mon ami.* But to be safe, I suggest you trade the girl off with me from time to time so no one draws too many erroneous conclusions. We've never had a problem on the tour. I'd hate for gossip to ruin future trips."

"Believe me, so would I, particularly since I plan to bring my own group of students next year. I appreciate the word of warning, Don. Let's just play this one by ear and see what happens, shall we? I know I'm looking forward to picking up on the tricks you use to shepherd these kids around and still keep them happy. Your legend precedes you."

On the surface the tension had appeared to ease, but Gerard knew Donald Bowen was smoldering with frustration beneath that calm facade.

"Thank you for *le compliment, Monsieur Smith.*"

"*De rien, Monsieur Bowen.* From all I hear, it's well deserved."

He cocked his dark head. "Your accent. You sound like you've spent time in Geneva."

"Lausanne, actually, but you were close." Gerard took the greatest of pleasure in correcting the other man. "I've been trying to place yours. You must have been in Belgium. There are certain sounds you make I've only heard in Charleroi."

After a brief silence, "You have an amazing ear. It's true I studied French there for a time."

"Not so amazing," Gerard denied. "I did a lot of skiing in Europe when I was much younger. One of my friends came from Charleroi. You sound very much like him when you talk. I'm surprised you don't plan a side trip to Belgium with your students.''

"They refuse to visit that part of Europe. All they really want to do is buy things in Paris and Switzerland. They don't care about the stained-glass windows of the Saint-Chappelle, or the Roman ruins around Lake Geneva.''

Evidently the man had decided to make small talk in the hope Gerard would forget how adamant he'd been about trading Ms. Lawrence for his own nefarious purposes.

"All American students are the same. Spoiled and shockingly carefree.''

"You're right about that,'' Donald muttered without humor.

"I'm afraid I was the same at their age. Where did you grow up?''

"Washington State. Bellevue. And you?''

So many lies, Monsieur Bowen. How do you keep track of them?

"Right here in Salt Lake. But I spent all my free time at our cabin in Alta, skiing and rock climbing.''

"My wife's family is from Salt Lake, Orem, to be precise. Between responsibilities at home and my profession, there hasn't been much time for sports the last few years.''

"I was married once myself, so I understand how the commitment cuts down on your free time. It's ideal you can take these trips to keep up your French.''

"That's why I go.''

"I'd like to keep my French current, as well. It's an excellent way to stay in touch with the students and use the language. Now if you'll excuse me, I'm going to get that drink before the show ends.''

"Of course."

"I've enjoyed our chat, Don. Fortunately we're going to have lots of time during the tour to do more of the same."

The other man nodded. "If I don't see you again tonight, we'll meet at the airport."

"Are you one of Mr. Smith's students?"

The film had ended and everyone was getting out of their seats. "Yes, ma'am," Whitney said on purpose to make herself sound as young as possible.

She'd been expecting Ms. Ashton to say something because it was perfectly clear that the French teacher was more than a little interested in Mr. Smith and wanted to give Whitney a piece of her mind for temporarily thwarting her plans.

What was equally obvious to Whitney was his indifference to Ms. Ashton. Whitney actually felt sorry for the other woman who must have come on several tours hoping for a relationship with him. Too bad she hadn't caught on that he preferred defenseless teenage girls who couldn't help succumbing to his charm.

The appraisal he'd given Whitney in the other room earlier provided proof that she'd been chosen for his next conquest. Things couldn't be working out better.

Slowly she would allow him to believe that she'd fallen into his hands like a ripe plum. Near the end of the tour, when he thought he could maneuver her into his bedroom as he'd done Christine, she'd have all the documentation she needed to expose him.

As far as Whitney was concerned, this would be his

last trip with STI since she intended to monopolize and seduce him until she could bring him up on charges of attempting to compromise her. Then they'd have a talk about Christine and Greg.

"Why didn't you sit with the rest of his group?" Ms. Ashton questioned a little too sharply.

The woman has claws. Whitney decided it was time to unsheathe a set of her own.

"Hank was helping me with a problem that made us late." Taking a calculated risk she added, "I told him I hated disturbing everyone, but he said you wouldn't mind, that you were the motherly type, always willing to help out one more. I hope it's all right."

No woman wanted to be thought of as a motherly type by the man she fantasized about. The left-handed compliment could even be construed as cruel. But Whitney couldn't afford to waste any time. With a limit of ten days, she needed to stake out her territory *now*, thereby eliminating any possible complications down the road.

"Don't you think you should show him the proper respect and call him Mr. Smith?"

Uh-oh. "I tried to be polite, but he told me everyone calls him Hank and he expects me to use it."

A deadly silence followed. Whitney didn't dare look in the other woman's direction. Instead she stood up, ready to leave the auditorium.

The other woman also got to her feet. "He's a very busy teacher with a lot of responsibilities. You should be careful not to monopolize his time."

"I would never do that." Whitney spoke over her shoulder. "But my grandmother has already made arrangements for him to sit next to me throughout the tour because my best friend had to cancel at the last minute and I'm all alone.''

''I'm sure we can find a girl for you to pal around with.''

''If you did that, I wouldn't be able to come on the tour. My grandmother says I have to stick with my teacher or I can't go at all.''

''But that's abs—being unreasonable.'' She amended what she was about to say as they both filed into the hallway. *The woman was livid.* ''Surely she can't expect your chaperone to keep you company every minute of the trip!''

''Hank said he would enjoy taking care of me, and told me not to worry about anything.'' On a burst of inspiration she decided to add one more tiny lie. ''He admitted that with me around, it might keep older women from bothering him when we're out in public.'' *Especially if they saw him touch her like he'd done in the auditorium earlier.*

Whitney was still trembling from the feel of his hand on her back. More and more she understood why Christine had become enamoured of him. Maybe because they were half sisters, it explained why both of them were attracted to the same kind of sensuous man.

''He sort of reminds you of Arnold Schwarzenegger, only he's much more attractive, don't you think, Ms. Ashton?''

A teenager could go into ecstasy over a man and no one would think anything of it. But the female French teacher had to maintain her decorum no matter how much she wanted to put Whitney in her place.

The other woman appeared tied up in little knots and wasn't saying anything.

"Oh, I'm sorry. I wasn't thinking. Maybe you're not into movies, or else you're too old to enjoy the kind he plays in. Not my grandmother, of course. She was always a movie lover and can tell you the name of every single movie star who has ever been in show business."

On that note Whitney figured she'd done enough damage for one night. "Well, I've got to go. My ride will be out front waiting for me. See you on Sunday. Thanks again for being so nice to me. Good night."

CHAPTER THREE

"MR. SMITH?"

Whitney ran up to him at the gate, pretending to be out of breath. But one look at him in khakis that molded his powerful thighs, and a pale blue knit shirt outlining his well-defined chest, and her breathlessness became real.

"S-sorry I'm late. My friend's car wouldn't start. At the last second I had to call for a taxi."

"I thought your grandmother was here."

"No. She suffers from severe arthritis and doesn't go out unless she can help it."

"That's too bad. I was hoping to meet her."

"There was no time, but she's planning to get a friend to drive her to Salt Lake at the end of the tour. She'll be there in her wheelchair, the first one to greet me off the plane and thank you for taking such good care of me."

Along with the lies, Whitney had once again delayed her arrival on purpose. For one thing, she hadn't wanted Mr. Smith to get a look at her passport when the person at the airline counter asked to see it. For another, she preferred to avoid any unnecessary conversation with Jeff and Roger while they stood in line to check their bags for the flight.

Last but not least, she knew Mr. Smith would watch for her no matter how late it got. It was part of his job as chaperone. The more ways she could contrive to keep them together without outside interference, the more proof she would be able to gather for her plan to expose him.

"As long as you got here," he murmured, yet he didn't sound angry or put out. Most teachers would have been furious by now. She wondered if his good nature was part of the facade to win over his unsuspecting victims.

"Come on, Whitney. They're going to close the doors on us." For no accountable reason the use of her first name sent a curious shiver down her spine. Without asking permission, he reached for her shoulder bag so she would only have to carry her camera case.

The perfect gentleman.

Christine had said that the man who'd made love to her had been wonderful. Whitney hated to admit it, but so far she had to agree with her sister.

Together they hurried onto the plane. He led her to two vacant seats at the back near the rest room and relieved her of her camera so she could sit down. From her vantage point the chartered DC-10 looked packed to the brim. *Like the proverbial sardines.*

"The bulk of the students coming on the tour loaded in Los Angeles." He read her mind with uncanny accuracy. "I'm afraid you lost your window seat by the wing. When the attendant thought you weren't coming, he gave it to another student. We'll have to sit here for the duration of the flight to Paris."

Nothing could have suited her more perfectly. At the rear of the plane no one would notice them. She could monopolize his time until he let down his guard and began showing his hand.

"You shouldn't have given up your seat to wait for me, Mr. Smith. I didn't expect preferential treatment on the plane. Nothing bad is going to happen to me here. At the meeting the other night, I only meant that I wanted to sit by you on the bus."

"Don't worry about it. While you fasten your seat belt, I'm going forward and let the boys know all is well."

While Whitney did his bidding, she drew pleasure from watching his striking, well-honed physique as he made his way up the aisle. To her chagrin, she found she had trouble concentrating on anything else but him. She was beginning to feel like the starry-eyed teenager she was impersonating.

But as soon as he was out of sight, she remembered that this man had taken advantage of her sister and had given her a baby. The recollection jerked Whitney back to the purpose of her mission and she renewed her vow to make him face up to his responsibilities.

"Ms. Lawrence?"

Deep in thought, it barely impinged on her consciousness that someone had called her name.

"Whitney Lawrence?"

She turned her head toward the aisle to find Mr. Bowen, Christine's French teacher, addressing her. He must have just boarded the plane himself.

"Yes?"

"I'm Donald Bowen, one of the French teachers going on your tour."

"Yes, I know who you are."

He gave her a pleasant smile. "I heard from the STI people that you wanted to join my group but were turned down. I'm sorry you were told that."

"It's all right, Mr. Bowen. I was assigned to Mr. Smith. Everything's fine."

"Nevertheless, I've made arrangements for you to be with us. If you'll come with me, I'll show you where my students are sitting. I have three girls who would love a fourth to even things up."

This was a development she hadn't counted on. But according to Christine, Mr. Bowen was a good friend to his students as well as a terrific teacher. Obviously he was trying to be nice because he'd just heard that Whitney had asked to be part of his group and had been turned down.

On the heels of that thought came another one. *Maybe Mr. Bowen had observed her chaperone on other trips. Maybe he knew about Mr. Smith's proclivity for teenage girls and was trying to protect her.*

If that were true, then she appreciated what he was attempting to do for her. But if she changed her seat now, she'd lose a singular opportunity to get close to the man who'd compromised her sister. Fourteen hours was a long time to be closeted together, so to speak. Anything could happen. That was exactly what she was hoping for.

"Thank you for thinking of me, but I'd better wait and discuss this with Mr. Smith."

"Discuss *what?*"

The deep, familiar male voice could only belong to one man. His tone of voice charged the air. Whitney's head whipped around to see Mr. Smith standing in the aisle, topping Mr. Bowen by several inches. With those fascinating gray-green eyes, he cast both of them a shrewd regard.

"Mr. Bowen was just telling me I should go forward and sit with the girls in his group, but the plane's ready to take off and I think it's too late to make changes now.''

"I couldn't agree with you more.''

She felt her heart begin to thud. *Mr. Smith doesn't want me to move. My plan is working.*

Her chaperone had been careful at the gate not to peruse her too intimately, but more than ever she sensed the strong physical chemistry between them. Certainly she would never forget the look of male desire she'd seen in his eyes the other night. She could still remember his hand on the back of her waist. It had felt natural. *It had felt right.*

She switched her glance to the other teacher. "Maybe on the flight home we can come up with other arrangements. Is that all right with you, Mr. Bowen?''

A fatherly expression dominated his features. "Of course. I just wanted you to know you don't have to feel left out.''

He was certainly living up to the qualities Christine had described in glowing terms.

"Thank you so much, Mr. Bowen.''

"You're entirely welcome. If you like, when we arrive in Paris we can switch things around on the bus so you won't have to be alone.''

"You're very kind to care.''

"Not at all. See you when we land. *Bon voyage.*''

Though it was his last instinct, Gerard gave the other man a friendly nod—as if their prior conversation in the library foyer had never taken place—and sat down next to Whitney.

After returning to his seat and discovering that

Donald Bowen had all but salivated over his young student, several things struck him forcefully.

The man would not rest until he'd managed to get to know Whitney a great deal better.

Even more clear to Gerard was Ms. Lawrence's intractability during what he imagined should have been a rather uncomfortable moment for her. Showing surprising backbone by not letting Donald Bowen manipulate her, Gerard saw a side to her nature that didn't correspond to his image of a fluffy-minded, immature teenager.

She handled the other man so well, it was getting more and more difficult to think of her as anything but a woman. One who, moreover, possessed a mystifying knowledge of how to treat the male of the species.

The impression that he was dealing with an equal intensified during takeoff when she didn't refer to the incident or act in the least nervous about the long flight ahead of them. The opposite of a chatty teen, once they'd achieved cruising speed, she took advantage of the time to read a magazine.

She'd made a promise to be good and leave him alone. It seemed she was determined to keep her word. What troubled Gerard was his inability to concentrate on the only reason for taking this trip in the first place.

He shouldn't have been pleased that Whitney had thwarted Donald Bowen's efforts to influence her. If anything, Gerard should have welcomed a chance to sit by the other man and get inside his head during the flight. Throughout the long trip over the ocean, he might have been able to pick up on the odd piece of information while the two of them conversed.

But chances were, the other man would use most of

the time to sleep. Under those conditions, nothing of real significance would be revealed. Once they landed in Paris, it would be a different matter and Gerard would have his work cut out watching and waiting until his target made a mistake.

For that reason Gerard had let Whitney dictate where she would sit on the plane. *At least that was what he'd been telling himself.*

As a result he now found himself seated next to her, a captive audience. Though their legs and arms didn't touch, he could feel her warmth, smell her perfume. Whenever she moved in her seat or let out a sigh, he was painfully aware of her physical proximity.

She was dressed in typical teenage garb of jeans and tailored blouse, yet he found himself envisioning her in a black evening dress. All that shiny abundance of ash-blond hair cried out for such a foil.

From the corner of his eye he could see her long, shapely legs and imagine them encased in the sheerest black hose. He could imagine too many things…

Alarmed at how much and how readily she occupied his thoughts, he realized that if he kept this up, his ability to get the proof he needed on Donald Bowen could be in serious jeopardy.

Gerard couldn't think of a more appropriate time than now to check in with Roman and keep him posted.

He pulled out his cell phone and punched in the office number, knowing it was Sunday, but hoping Roman might be in anyway. Phil answered, letting him know he was the only one around. Gerard told him not to bother Roman who needed to spend time alone with his wife. He said he'd call at the house later, then he clicked off.

Aware that Whitney didn't seem to be reading the magazine article any longer, he turned to her. "Would you like to phone your grandmother and tell her you're all right?"

For an instant, their gazes collided. The natural light in the cabin intensified the amazing lavender-blue hue of her irises fringed by dark lashes. A man could get lost in them.

After a moment's hesitation she looked away and shook her head. "An offer like that is very tempting, but I'm watching every penny and can't afford to be beholden to you. I'll send her some postcards from Paris as soon as we get to our hotel. Thank you again anyway, Mr. Smith."

If he'd asked Jeff or Roger, they would have taken him up on his offer. But he had to remember he was dealing with Whitney Lawrence. There was nothing predictable about her. Among her many qualities he could add manners and class. Her grandmother had raised her well.

He put his phone away. "Call me Hank. Every time you say Mr. Smith, I feel a year older."

"Ms. Ashton warned me that it wasn't fitting for me to be that casual with you."

The quiet admission made him grimace. "What else did she say to you?" It might be wise to hear the rest. He began to suspect that Fran and Donald had been collaborating against him to further their own ends.

"It wasn't that important."

Ms. Lawrence was a lady, too. As far as Gerard could tell, there was absolutely nothing wrong with her except for the fact that she was an untouchable eighteen-year-old.

"I'd really like to know, Whitney. After all, I'm your chaperone for this trip. If you want to get the most out of the tour, then we can't afford to have any misunderstandings between us."

Her hands tightened on the magazine, proof that the experience with Fran hadn't been particularly pleasant.

"She said something about not monopolizing your time. I—I think she likes you a lot and must have talked to Mr. Bowen about it."

Good Lord. Whitney Lawrence was nobody's fool. How did she manage to acquire so much wisdom in her few short years?

"It's probably why he asked me to sit with his group." She went on talking. "I'm afraid I've made things awkward for you. When we get to France, I'll sit with whomever you teachers decide. Just don't let my grandmother know."

The tremor in her voice found an answering chord in him. It was ludicrous that a sweet, intelligent, young woman like Whitney had been made the focal point of a lot of ugliness. He'd be damned if he would allow it to continue.

"I offered to let you sit with me throughout the bus tour. Have you changed your mind?"

"No," she asserted with enough emotion to satisfy him that she was telling the truth. "I just didn't want to be a nuisance to you, Mr. Smith."

I wish you were *a nuisance. I could deal with that...*

"I doubt you've ever been a problem to anybody, Whitney. But I *will* get upset if you don't start calling me Hank."

"If you want, I'll call you Hank when we're alone like this."

I wonder how affable you would be if you ever found yourself really alone with a man twice your age...

When Gerard realized how far his thoughts had wandered, he raked a hand through his hair in self-disgust. "That sounds the perfect compromise. What are you reading that has captured your attention for so long?"

"Oh, the magazine has an interesting article on the Élysées Palace in Paris. Apparently some rarely seen rooms are going to be opened up to the public during June. Naturally it's not on our itinerary. It's too bad we're only going to be in Paris a few days. There's so much to see and so little time to do everything."

Gerard shouldn't have been surprised that she was knowledgeable about the less frequented landmarks of the famous French capital. He wondered about her ability to converse in French.

"Parlez-vous Français, mademoiselle?"

"Pas comme vous, monsieur," she responded with a typical American accent.

Her answer delighted him. He couldn't prevent the chuckle that escaped. When she turned to look at him, the corners of her exquisitely sculpted mouth were on the verge of a smile.

"Is my French that bad?"

"Not at all. It was your answer that amused me."

"Why?"

"The usual response to 'Do you speak French?' is, 'A little bit.' But you came back with, 'Not like

you do, sir.' No one has ever made that particular remark to me before.''

He chuckled again, unable to help himself. She was
like a breath of fresh air in more ways than one.

''I said it on purpose so you would understand my
French is awful. That's one of the reasons I'm so
happy I'm going to be sitting by you on the tour. I
can listen to you speak and try to imitate you. You'll
be my living language laboratory. I'm afraid I didn't
use the language lab at our school as often as I should
have.''

''A lab helps, but there's no substitute for living in
Europe and becoming immersed in the language.''

''Is that what you did?''

''Yes.''

''Where?''

''Germany, Austria, France, Switzerland,
Belgium.''

''You were very fortunate. I always wanted to see
Switzerland.''

''Any particular reason?'' To his surprise, the re-
minder of another life with Simone no longer brought
him pain, only a treasured memory.

''When I was younger, I inherited a miniature
wooden Swiss village for Christmas. There were lots
of little chalets, churches, buildings and barns. Inside
I found tiny people dressed in native costume, plus
cows with cow bells, and St. Bernard dogs carrying
little barrels you could fill with juice. One of the
churches contained a music box. It played a Swiss
mountain tune.

''The village was designed to scale from a town on
Lake Geneva called Montreux. It was so adorable, I

fell in love with it on sight and played with it every day. My friends thought I was mean because I wouldn't let them touch it, but I was afraid one of them might damage it.

"I vowed that when I grew up, I'd travel to Switzerland and see the real town for myself. That's why I took French in the first place. Have you ever been to Montreux?'' Her earnest gaze darted to his once more.

"Many times.'' Her description had enchanted him. "It's called the jewel of Lac Leman.''

"I wish our tour were going there, but I know we can't see everything.''

"Maybe something can be arranged,'' he murmured.

"I don't think so.''

"Not for the whole bus certainly. But it's possible you could get away from the regular tour for the day and return to the group in the evening.''

"Not alone.'' Her voice trembled.

"Naturally someone would have to accompany you.''

"I wouldn't want to put anyone out.''

"Why don't we wait until we reach Geneva and see what can be arranged.''

She bit her lip. "Both cities are on the same lake, aren't they?''

"That's right. Too bad we're not traveling to Switzerland in the fall. At that time of year there are wildflowers in bloom on the hillsides above Montreux the exact color of your eyes.''

The second the words were out Gerard realized his mistake, but the damage had already been done.

Instead of blushing or turning her head as an embarrassed young person might do, she continued to look at him through half-veiled eyes. "No one ever made that comparison before."

"Then we've both surprised each other today."

As recognition dawned, her mouth widened into a smile that reached a core deep inside him. Suddenly he experienced an inexplicable explosion of excitement that coursed through his veins like an adrenaline rush, only much headier.

What are you doing, Roche? What in the hell is wrong with you? She's a teenager.

"Excuse me, sir. We're serving breakfast. Would you care for coffee, tea, milk or cranberry juice?"

Gerard hadn't even noticed the steward. "Coffee, please. Black."

"And you, miss?"

"Juice, please."

For the next little while Whitney occupied herself with enjoying her breakfast in silence, content in the knowledge that Mr. Smith was going to be a pushover to set up. He'd already compared the color of her eyes to flowers. No doubt his mind was busy planning the big seduction scene in Montreux. She could hardly wait until his *denouement* began.

Little did he know she was wearing a mini microrecorder behind the collar of her blouse. It had picked up every incriminating word he'd spoken since greeting her at the gate.

Too bad the microphone couldn't pick up the man's unforgettable looks or his incredible masculine sex appeal. But it did capture that amazing line of his, a silken line so long it could reach around the world twice, and make any girl or woman feel she was the only person on earth.

Soon she would get him to start talking about his fictitious personal life, his fictitious estranged wife and his poor little fictitious daughter who by now was supposed to be five years old.

Whitney had made up the story about the Swiss village in the hope that he might talk about his child and the new toys he was planning to buy her on the trip. She presumed he always used the same story about his daughter to entrap his victims.

When the two of them reached Montreux—and they would because he would personally see to it—he would feign illness and require a hotel room to recover. Then she would be dispatched to pick up his child's gift. When Whitney returned, he would invite her into his room to thank her.

Perhaps after they enjoyed a drink together, one thing would lead to another and she'd have it all on tape, even his suggestion that they go to bed together.

At that point she would introduce herself as Christine's sister and inform him he had a son. Next she would tell him that every moment of their conversation since the start of the tour had been taped, and those tapes were in the hands of an attorney in Salt Lake.

Finally, if he dared to take the tape recorder she was wearing off her body, it wouldn't do him any good since she would have arranged for a policeman to block the door in case he tried to escape with it.

That would be the end of *Monsieur Smith's* teaching career, at least in the State of Utah.

Before long the steward came by to remove their breakfast trays. Whitney noticed that Mr. Smith had put his head back and had closed his eyes. Now that they'd eaten, she felt sleepy herself and followed suit.

About two hours later she awakened and decided to go visit the ladies' room. As she got out of her seat, she had to step past Mr. Smith's hard-muscled legs and couldn't resist another glance at the strong lines and angles of his facial features.

The sun must have lightened his dark-blond hair in the front, making an arresting contrast to his burnished skin. More than a suntan, she had the impression he spent a lot of his free time in the mountains, whether winter or summer.

She had to admit he was an exceptional male on many levels. Christine could be forgiven for getting involved with him. What Whitney found unforgivable was the man's penchant for teenage girls.

There were hundreds, thousands, of single, willing, available older women like Ms. Ashton who would love to date such an attractive man. *But he wasn't interested.*

Whitney was positive that if he'd known she was an attorney, and they'd met at a legitimate business lunch or some such affair, he wouldn't have given her the time of day. It made her sick how some young, innocent girls were exploited by men who looked and acted like him, but were loathesome monsters beneath their suave veneers.

Bitterness made her body stiffen before she looked away from him and set out for her destination more determined than ever to make him pay for his sins.

"Oh, no," she groaned inwardly as she emerged

from the rest room a few minutes later to find Ms. Ashton waiting for her. From the look of those dark brown eyes glaring at her beneath a fringe of dark brown bangs, something told Whitney this accidental meeting had been planned.

"Hi, Ms. Ashton."

"You did it again, didn't you."

The gloves were off. "I'm afraid I don't understand."

"Like hell you don't. You purposely came late like you did at the library meeting so you could monopolize Mr. Smith's time. But we're on to you, young lady, and we won't allow this tour to be ruined by a selfish, manipulative, spoiled little teenager like you. There's always one on every bus."

Whoa. Like Whitney's sister, Ms. Ashton could be forgiven for having it bad for Mr. Smith, but the woman was unconscionably cruel and ought not to be a teacher if she could treat a student like this.

"I'm not trying to cause any trouble," she answered back as sweetly as she could. "How could I help it that Mr. Smith would be waiting at the gate to get me on board? It certainly wasn't planned."

"Lie all you want, Whitney Lawrence. I can see right through you. Enjoy the flight, because when we arrive in Paris, things are going to change. Trust me on this one."

Whitney shook her head in feigned bewilderment. "What do you mean?"

"Don't put on that airheaded act for me. You've got the instincts of a predator. Think about it awhile and I'm sure the answer will come to you."

Without so much as an excuse me, she brushed past

Whitney in a fury and slammed the rest room door shut.

Schooling her features not to smile at so much pent-up frustration on the other woman's part, Whitney started back to her seat.

"Hi," Mr. Smith murmured as she found her place and sat down once more. "You were gone a long time. Are you all right?"

Whitney had a sudden flash of inspiration and kept her head slightly bowed, not looking at him.

"I—I'm okay."

"What's wrong?" The authoritative tone of his question told her he wouldn't let this go until he'd received the answer he wanted.

"I'd rather not talk about it."

"I saw Ms. Ashton headed for the rest room, Whitney. What did she say to upset you?"

"Please, Mr. Smith. It doesn't matter."

"It does to me. I'm your chaperone this trip and if you've got a problem, we need to discuss it."

"It's a girl thing."

"What do you mean?"

"Remember when I told you that other girls don't like me around for fear I'll take away their boyfriends?"

"I do."

Whitney lifted her head so he could see into her eyes, which were brimming with unshed tears. "Well, it isn't just girls who don't like me."

His features darkened. "Tell me what she said to you *exactly*."

"I told you before. She's made it no secret that she likes you a lot. She's angry at me because she thinks

I manipulated things so I could sit by you on the plane.''

Whitney had injected just the right amount of wobble in her voice, as if she were fighting not to break down in front of him. ''Mr. Smith—I mean, Hank.'' She'd purposely waited to use his first name until now for its sheer impact value. ''Maybe I shouldn't have come on this trip at all.''

CHAPTER FOUR

"WHITNEY?"

"Yes?" came a whisper veiled in tears.

"Take my advice and forget what's happened."

"That's hard to do."

"You're not alone, you know. I'm here and I'll make certain no one bothers you anymore."

A long silence ensued. Then he heard a quiet, "Thank you."

"You're welcome. Why don't you try to sleep again. I'll wake you when they serve lunch."

"I'd like that. I was up all last night cooking meals to put in the freezer for my grandmother so she wouldn't have to worry about preparing a lot of food while I'm gone. I guess I'm more tired than I realized."

Her concern for her grandmother touched Gerard deeply. He reached for one of the pillows above their heads and handed it to her.

"Thank you." She took it from him. "How did I get so lucky?" The wet eyes she raised to him shimmered like rare amethysts.

He felt his chest constrict. "What do you mean?"

"You're a wonderful man. I've never met anyone like you. For the first time in my life, I feel…safe. Cherished. It's the best feeling in the world."

Then her eyelids closed and she sank back into the pillow. He watched her for a moment, mesmerized by her words and the aura of inner beauty that paralleled her physical attributes.

Fran Ashton's jealousy was easily understandable. Even so, Gerard wondered if Whitney weren't being manipulated between Fran and Donald Bowen like a pawn in an elaborate chess game.

In light of the uncalled-for focus on Whitney, Gerard's theory that Donald could be using a female student to accomplish his objective was taking on more and more credibility. Maybe Fran was a plant who worked with him to zero in on the most likely female candidate and coerce her into making and picking up deliveries containing sensitive material.

If on each trip Donald resorted to seducing one of his female students *first* as the standard operating method of getting her into his power, then it only made sense the lowlife would pick the most appealing girl to sign up for the tour.

Whitney Lawrence won that contest hands down.

If Gerard's theory was right, then Donald must be seething by now because Ms. Lawrence hadn't been cooperating like his former students had done in the past. Otherwise he wouldn't still be in business.

So far, Whitney had shown amazing courage by standing up to both adults. Something told Gerard that even without the protection he'd given her so far, Whitney would have balked at their intimidation tactics. She had an independent spirit. He'd seen her in action. Up to this point she had refused to be patronized.

He couldn't help but admire that trait in her. Yet because of that *exact* quality, he had a hard time remembering she wasn't his equal in all the other ways that counted. Except for her clothes, she didn't look or act like a teenager. She presented a baffling mystery. *Face it, Gerard. Your attraction to her is more than skin deep.*

Because of that attraction, he was having a hard time separating his emotional response from the facts in the case.

Was his justifiable anger over her precarious situation coming from his personal feelings? Would he have felt this protective of her if he hadn't been affected by the almost overpowering chemistry between them?

He didn't have answers to those questions, but he did know one thing. Donald Bowen would never be allowed to get his tainted hands on her. *Not even close.*

It had been a long time since Gerard had felt this kind of rage against another human in his line of work. But nothing got to him more than to see a man who used his age and power to prey on the young and the helpless.

Whitney Lawrence was by no means helpless, but she had unknowingly walked into a trap and was up against a cold-blooded professional who would let nothing stand in the way of achieving his goal.

Fran Ashton's part in the scheme of things was still questionable. All he needed to do was phone the right party, and he would have answers by the time they reached Paris.

After another quick look at Whitney who had followed his advice to try and sleep, he levered himself from the seat and went to the rest room to make the call.

Once the door was locked, he pulled out his cell

phone and punched in Roman's home number. Brittany's cheery voice answered on the third ring. After greeting him warmly, she said she'd take the phone to her husband who was in the shower. Gerard could hear their baby making happy noises in the background.

"You're a blessed man," Gerard murmured as Roman came on the line.

"Tell me about it," his boss responded just as emotionally. "What's going on?"

"Since I hate interrupting you and your wife on a Sunday, I'll make this short. I need a background check on a Fran Ashton. She could be named Frances, Francine, maybe even Francesca. I want anything and everything you can find. It's possible she's Bowen's accomplice. She's a French teacher at Rosemont High in the Valley School District."

"I'll get right on it."

"Won't Brittany mind?"

"No. I had already planned to run to the office for a few hours to do some work on another case. She's going to take Yuri for a visit to his grandparents. Later in the day we'll be going on a picnic up the canyon."

"Like I said, you're one fortunate *Ruskie*."

"Hey, *Comrade*. Are the memories starting to get to you after all?"

At times, Roman's intuition was uncanny.

"No." Gerard's emphatic answer surprised even himself. "To be honest, my mind hasn't been on the past." *Not at all.* Another startling truth for which he had no explanation.

"Well, it's evident that something's wrong. Why do

I have the feeling it doesn't have anything to do with Donald Bowen?''

He ground his teeth. "You're right. It doesn't.''

"You want to talk about it?''

"*Lord,* Roman— There's thi—''

A tap on the door prevented him from saying anything more. Maybe it was just as well. How in the hell could he admit to Roman that he was attracted to a girl who was young enough to be his offspring? He couldn't believe the intensity of his feelings after so short a time. None of it made sense.

He lowered his voice to a hushed whisper. "Someone's here. I can't talk now. I'll phone you before we land in Paris. Maybe by then you'll have some news for me.''

"You can count on it. Maybe by then you'll be able to spill your guts to me. I've been there. Remember, *Comrade?*''

"I do.'' Gerard took a steadying breath. "Thanks. I may take you up on it. Over and out.''

Gerard clicked off and opened the door. Anxious to get back to Whitney, he brushed past one of the male students waiting outside. The last few incidents had made him paranoid to leave her alone. But his fears that Donald Bowen might have taken the opportunity to bother her again proved to be unfounded.

When he returned to his seat, she was sleeping soundly. Under the circumstances he thought it would be a good time to check on Jeff and Roger.

While moving forward in the aisle, he happened to pass Fran's gregarious group. She darted him a furtive glance. Instead of acknowledging his greeting, she looked away again with a perceptible chiseling of her features.

Her reaction was more typical of a woman who knew she'd been rejected and was hurt by it. An agent wouldn't have allowed personal feelings to show or interfere. It caused him to rethink his hunch that she might be working with Donald.

Then again, she might be a master spy playing the perfect part of the rebuffed woman to throw him off the scent. Whatever the true answer, he wasn't about to take any chances. Once he'd learned what Roman's research had uncovered, he would decide how to handle Fran for the rest of the tour.

"Monsieur Smith?"

"Bonjour, Roger. Salut, Jeff."

They both answered in kind. "Where's Whitney? We thought she'd come to say hi by now."

"She's asleep, but I have no doubts she'll want to walk around after lunch. Are you enjoying the flight so far? Since we left the Rockies, it's been smooth as glass."

Jeff frowned. "It's boring."

"Yeah, and there aren't any girls around to compare to Whitney. She's hot! You know what we mean?"

I'm very much afraid that I do, Roger. "When we get to France, you're going to find out there are lots of attractive French girls for you to admire." He winked.

Both teens chuckled and nodded their heads. They were intelligent and nice. Gerard was impressed with them and grateful he'd inherited a couple of male students who wouldn't cause any problems.

"In case you guys need anything, come and find me at the rear of the plane. *À bientôt* for now."

"See ya, Mr. Smith. And tell Whitney we want to talk to her."

"I'll do that."

At least the boys' reactions to Whitney were normal and healthy. *Not like mine,* he muttered in self-deprecation. You're nothing but a *lecher,* Gerard.

Whitney had reams of material she should be reading in connection with a troubled restaurant franchise case she was dealing with back at her corporate law firm, but under no circumstances could she afford to let Mr. Smith catch her indulging in her occupation.

Lunch had been over ages ago and she needed to do something or go stir crazy. She thought of getting into a novel she'd bought at the airport gift shop, but she couldn't seem to concentrate. It disturbed her that the man lounging in the next seat took up all of her thoughts.

He was the enemy, she had to keep reminding herself.

If they were in a court of law, he'd be sitting at the opposite table with his defense attorney fighting a losing battle.

Mr. Smith *was* going to lose because she could produce a living witness who would testify that he had no principles. Since Whitney knew that, *why* was she having such a hard time believing it?

Because he's good at what he does. So good, in fact, you'd better be careful he doesn't get to you, too.

Upset at the trend of her thoughts, she reached for the crossword puzzle magazine she'd purchased.

Turning to the difficult section at the back, she immersed herself in deciphering the definitions of obscure words. For the next few hours it provided a much needed distraction.

"Stuck on a word?"

Apparently he'd been watching her. It was paying off to leave him alone. However, there was one problem. When he did speak, his low, vibrant voice produced an involuntary quickening of her body. That reaction wasn't supposed to happen.

Where he was concerned, *there wasn't supposed to be any reaction at all.*

She'd been acting out this elaborate charade to catch him and make him pay for what he'd done to Christine. So what was wrong with her that she was getting emotionally involved?

"I've done the whole puzzle except for one item that needs ten letters."

"What's the definition?"

"'Additional territory deemed necessary to a nation.'" I keep thinking annexation, but the word is supposed to end in an 'm.'"

"Mind if I take a look?"

"Not at all."

She handed him the magazine. In the process, their fingers brushed against each other. Licks of fire shot through her hands and up her arms, but she had to pretend his touch hadn't affected her. After a moment, he gave it back.

"Try lebensraum."

She asked him to spell it. When he did, the word fit perfectly. "I've never heard of it. Lebensraum sounds German."

He nodded. "It's a term often associated with the Nazi's."

"Do you speak German, too?"

"Yes. My father came from Heidelberg, my mother from Lausanne."

"But you sound totally American."

"That's because I was born and raised in Utah."

"Where exactly?"

"Salt Lake. But all of my free time was spent at my parents' cabin in the Peruvian basin in Alta."

Whitney's favorite place to ski. It seemed to her that if he'd really been up there, she would have noticed him in the ski lines or on the slopes. He'd be impossible to miss. It was just another lie.

"When did you go off to Europe?"

"At eighteen. Just like you. I stayed with various relatives and graduated from university there."

"You've had an amazing life so far. I hope this doesn't sound too personal, but are you married?"

"I was."

Was?

"Hank…you don't have to tell me anything else if you don't want to."

"You confided in me about living with your grandmother. It's only natural you would want to know something about my life. I was married, but no longer," came the vague response.

Oh, brother. Since being with Christine, he'd probably changed his story so his victims wouldn't feel guilty about having an affair with a married man.

She noticed that he'd deliberately left the rest of his comment to speculation. He was a real pro at this.

It was on the tip of her tongue to ask him about his

fictitious daughter, but she decided she'd asked enough questions for now. The rest could come later.

"I'm sorry. It must be awful for you. My grandfather died prematurely. I'm afraid my grandmother never got over it."

For a long interval he didn't say anything. Finally, "I'm sure that for older people, it's much more difficult to find yourself unexpectedly alone. I won't pretend it's been easy, but I've discovered that when I'm around young people, I feel better because their excitement is contagious."

I'll just bet it is.

"That's one of the reasons I decided to come on this tour."

And we both know what the other reason is. Little do you know you're as transparent as glass.

"Well, I'm certainly thankful you volunteered to be a chaperone. In fact, I don't know what I'd do without you now." She put just the right amount of throb into her voice, but it took all her willpower not to laugh.

"You won't have to find out, so don't worry about it."

Those are words to thrill a maiden's heart. You're a master at what you do, Mr. Smith.

"Maybe we can help each other?" she suggested in a shy tone.

"You already have."

"Are you talking about Ms. Ashton?"

He turned to her, eyeing her narrowly. "How did you know?"

"Because I've seen the way she looks at you. Forgive me, but you don't look at her the same way back. She must have heard you weren't married anymore. Maybe that's why she's disappointed you haven't paid more attention to her.''

''The attraction has to be mutual.''

''I know. It's the same reason I haven't gone forward to visit with Roger and Jeff. Nice as they are, I don't want them to get any ideas that I'm interested. The fact is, I'm not and never could be.

''For the time being I'm anxious to see a little of the world, and am perfectly content to experience Europe with a man of your sophistication. I know I'm going to learn a lot.''

Emboldened by his silence she said, ''Forgive me if I sounded outspoken just now about Ms. Ashton. My grandmother says it's a fault I need to work on.''

''It's a refreshing quality, not a fault, Whitney. You have a wisdom beyond your years that makes me tend to forget you're only eighteen.''

Really. Now we're getting to the part you used on Christine to break her down.

''Men always think I'm older, probably because they're the only ones who try to get to know me. As I said before, girls are always afraid I'm going to infringe on their territory, so they set up barriers to keep me out. But I've learned to compensate for their rejection in other ways.''

''Does that mean a special boyfriend?''

''No. I've never been able to relate to guys my own age. They're too immature. You're probably thinking I am, too.''

Taking advantage of the fact that his gaze was still on her, she sighed and stretched as provocatively as she dared. When she looked at him again, his gray eyes were glittering with a strange green light that caused her breath to catch. *Another reaction inside her she couldn't seem to control.*

"On the contrary." His voice grated. "You're not anything like the others."

The tension between them had become electric.

Whitney started to tremble. She knew when a man wanted her. Desire wasn't something you could fake. This man showed all the signs. She could sense it, feel it.

There was another problem, even more serious. Despite the whole purpose of this vendetta against him, there was a part of her that wanted him, too. So much so, she could taste it.

Something was wrong here. Terribly, terribly wrong.

"Hey, Whitney?" a voice called out. "They're starting to serve dinner already. How come you haven't been to see us? We've been waiting all day."

Jolted out of her dazed condition, she turned her head to discover Jeff in the aisle. For once, Roger hadn't accompanied him.

"Hi, Jeff. I just woke up. I guess I've been more tired than I realized."

In the next instant Mr. Smith had risen to his feet. "Sit down for a while, Jeff, and have dinner with Whitney. After I stretch my legs, I'll eat with Roger."

"Are you sure?"

"Bien sûr."

A smile wreathed his face. "Thanks, Hank."

Stifling a moan, Whitney watched him disappear down the aisle. She understood why he'd allowed Jeff some time with her. This way none of the teachers in their group could accuse him of monopolizing her time or vice versa.

What she didn't understand was this tumult of unexplained feelings he engendered in spite of everything bad she knew about him.

"He's cool, isn't he?"

Cool? Oh, Jeff. You poor thing. You don't have a clue what's going on here. *Unfortunately, neither do I.*

The charter flight would be landing at Orly airport outside Paris within the hour. Gerard had stayed forward with Roger through dinner and a movie, then excused himself. Before there was a rush on the rest rooms, he found a vacant one to make the next phone call to Roman.

His boss answered after the second ring.

"What have you got for me, Roman?"

"You'll know better than I if anything sounds suspicious, but I'd say she's clean. Named Francine Mallory Ashton, born to Ira and Lucille Mallory Ashton from Murray, Utah. Raised in Murray, attended Murray High School, received her B.A. degree in French education from Westminster College in Salt Lake.

"Did a French summer workshop in Quebec, Canada, with other teachers from Westminster. In case you were trying to make a connection, Interpol has established that Donald Bowen never attended Westminster, and can furnish proof he was in France and Switzerland at the same time she was in Canada.

"Taught junior high French one year in Alpine, Utah. Has taught French four years at Rosemont High

School. She's never been married. Lives in an apartment with a female physical education teacher. She took out a passport three years ago to travel with STI, and has made three student/teacher trips to France and Switzerland with them in the summers.

"There have been no driving citations or outstanding warrants for her arrest. She drives a used Honda Civic registered in Salt Lake County. She files her income tax every year, on time. Her gross income is $36,000. She's an active member of the Valley and Utah Education Association. Is not a member of any known activist groups of any kind. She attends the Presbyterian Church."

Gerard had been listening intently. "You're right, Roman. Everything sounds pretty straightforward. If there's a connection and she's working for him, then he probably recruited her after they met through their association in the Valley School District."

"What else can I do for you?"

"Donald Bowen says he was born in Seattle, Washington, that his wife was from Orem, Utah. He admits attending school in Charleroi, Belgium, which is the only thing he told me that might have some veracity."

"I'll check it out. Anything else?"

Whitney's image, her intelligence, the way she expressed herself refused to leave his mind. It was a good thing Jeff had come along when he did. Gerard had been enjoying her company far too much. If he didn't know she was eighteen, he would place her anywhere from twenty-five to thirty years old.

"*Comrade?* Are you still there?"

"*Ja.*"

"I've got time if you do."

"You're a good man, Roman."

"My instincts tell me you've met a woman."

A groan escaped. *Whitney was all woman.* "As usual, your instincts are right on."

"Is it Fran Ashton?"

"*Lord,* I wish it were!"

"Are you saying it's one of your students?"

"I swear nothing like this has ever happened to me before."

"Some eighteen-year-olds can be very mature for their age. I take it her attraction for you is equally strong."

He sucked in his breath. "That part is easy to explain. It's hero worship, Roman, nothing more. Whitney Lawrence has always lived with her grandmother up in Box Elder County. There's been no male role model in the home.

"She's one of those straight-A students who has always had to earn her money if she wanted something. This trip represents being on her own for the first time in her life. She's totally innocent and vulnerable. The problem lies with me and what I'm feeling." He raked an unsteady hand through his hair.

"What exactly are you feeling?"

"What *aren't* I feeling might be a better way to describe my condition." His voice shook.

After a pause, "You're serious, aren't you?"

"*Hell,* Roman. Remember how you felt about Brittany the first time you met her?"

Another silence ensued. "You should have dated someone else after Annabelle."

"It wouldn't have mattered if I'd dated a dozen

women. Whitney's so different, you'd have to see her
and talk to her to understand why I'm in turmoil.''

"Look, Gerard— If you don't think you can keep
emotional or physical distance from her, then Interpol
needs to line up another teacher who can meet your
plane in Paris and take your place for the rest of the
tour.''

''I've been thinking about doing just that for the
last couple of hours, but things are getting compli-
cated. Donald Bowen is all over Whitney right now. I
know he wants to get her into his bed, but I also think
he plans to use her to pass information, probably to
some Middle Eastern faction.''

"So *that's* how he does it.''

"I'd stake my career on it.''

"Trust you to figure things out this fast. What
tipped you off?''

"Bowen hasn't left Whitney alone since the meeting at the library. She was supposed to have been assigned to him, but his group was full so I inherited
her. Now he wants her back and has been fairly ruthless about it. He acts driven, which is the reason I've
grown suspicious.

"At first I thought maybe she was a plant, that she
had disguised herself as a teenager to help Bowen as
soon as the two of them reached Europe. But after
getting to know her, I dismissed that theory.''

"Never disregard a theory no matter how much you
might not like it or how much it doesn't make sense.
The few times I ignored what I presumed was an in-
consequential idea, I lived to regret it.''

"I hear you.''

"Why don't I check her out, just to be on the safe side."

Part of Gerard rebelled against the idea.

"If you're hesitating, it means you're still entertaining reservations about her."

"Oh, hell, Roman. I don't know what I think. She doesn't look or act like an eighteen-year-old, but appearances can be deceiving."

"That's true. What high school did she attend?"

"Union. She graduated with a four point grade average."

"Her last name's Lawrence?"

"Right."

"Give me a description."

Gerard's eyes closed tightly. "She's five-nine, five-ten, medium-length ash-blond hair, lavender-blue eyes."

"Body type?"

"Voluptuous."

"Any marks or scars?"

"None. She has flawless skin. Flawless *everything*."

"I'm beginning to understand your dilemma," Roman muttered.

"You don't know the half of it." The scent of her skin, the way she breathes when she talks, the movement of her body, those firm, shapely legs that go on forever. Gerard had thought the attraction for his wife had been intense... "I'll phone you from the hotel in Paris, probably eight hours from now."

"Good. That will give me enough time to check on her and Bowen."

"Roman—"

"I know. No matter what we learn about her, the answer's going to be unpalatable."

"You got it in one." His voice rasped.

"Like I said, you can be replaced and come on back home."

When Gerard had taken this assignment, there was always the possibility that memories of Simone might interfere with his concentration.

But what he hadn't counted on was being forced to return to Salt Lake because of an attraction to an eighteen-year-old girl. The fear was growing that he wouldn't be able to keep his hands off her. He'd never come up against a situation like this in his professional career. Talking to Roman seemed to help him come to a conclusion.

"If it turns out she's who she says she is, I'll be on the first plane home."

He could hear Roman reading between the lines. "Since I don't want you getting into any trouble, *Comrade,* I'll contact Interpol and alert them to have someone else ready to take over for you by tomorrow morning, if necessary."

CHAPTER FIVE

"BONJOUR tout le monde. Soyez le bienvenu à Paris.
Welcome to Paris. I am Jean-Luc, your tour guide and
liaison with Student Teacher International.

"This is Enrico, your bus driver. We will be your
family on wheels for the next eight days. Anything
you need, you talk to us.

"Your hotel rooms will not be ready before two
o'clock in the afternoon. Until that time, we will follow the itinerary and enjoy a morning tour to the for-
ested town of Fontainebleau whose château we will
visit before we take a break for lunch. Your luggage
has been taken care of. Before we go, are there any
questions?"

While some of the students asked about changing
their money into francs, Whitney stayed close to Mr.
Smith and studied the two men who had been responsible for conducting Christine's tour the year before.

Jean-Luc had the dark looks of a typical Frenchman,
rather lean, medium height, a slightly Roman nose, his
age anywhere from thirty-five to forty.

Enrico had to be in his mid-forties to early fifties,
a short, wiry Italian with thinning brown hair and eyes,
whose body English was as expressive as the several
languages he spoke. A cigarette dangled continually
from his lips.

Having met Mr. Smith first, Whitney had dismissed
the idea that the tour guide or driver could have been

the father of Christine's baby. One look at the two foreign men and she realized more than ever that her sister couldn't possibly have been attracted to them.

As for the other male teachers traveling on their bus, they were too old to have interested any woman under the age of forty. Mr. Bowen hadn't quite reached that point, but he was getting there. Whitney found them all rather homely.

"Board the bus, please. *Montez, s'il vous plaît!*"

Needing no urging, every student including Roger and Jeff clamored to get on first so they could grab a seat in the rear. Not in any hurry to get crushed, Whitney waited for Mr. Smith to finish his conversation with one of the other teachers.

After the intimacy the plane afforded, it seemed odd to have to share him with other people. Literally the most attractive man around, *and the most attractive man she'd ever met,* Whitney noticed how the boys vied for his attention while the girls used one pretext or another to flirt with him.

She could easily picture Christine as one of those eager, excited teens dancing attendance on him. He had the charm and sophistication of an urbane host who put young and old at ease. Only Ms. Ashton, no longer enchanted with him, kept her distance. Whitney might have experienced more guilt for having sabotaged things if Mr. Smith hadn't told her that he didn't return the other woman's ardor.

In order to get on the bus, Whitney had to pass by the two men who stood outside the door speaking French while gesticulating with their hands.

"*Bonjour, mademoiselle.*" This from Jean-Luc

whose bold appraisal warned her she was in for more of the same unsolicited attention during the trip.

The Italian gave her a lopsided grin, eyeing her from tip to toe. *"Bellisima, signorina."*

Whitney had been forced to put up with the same male behavior when she'd been to Mexico on several spring vacations. This was nothing new, just irritating.

The tour guide's gaze dropped to the name tag pinned to her blouse. "Wheet-nee. That's a preetty name for a very beauteeful girl."

From somewhere behind her she heard Mr. Smith address both men in French. Whatever he said caused a change in them. They shrugged and left her alone.

During unpleasant moments like this, Whitney would be the first to admit she enjoyed a man's protection, but considering it was Mr. Smith, she was filled with irreconcilable conflicts. Could anything be more hypocritical than for him to chastise them for flirting with her when he had every intention of seducing her at the first opportunity?

"Let's get on, Whitney."

At his terse command, which secretly delighted her because it meant he was feeling territorial about her, she climbed on board only to discover that neither Jeff nor Roger had been able to save them seats. She was left with two options—either sit by Mr. Grimshaw or Mr. Bowen, who were both up in front on either side of the aisle.

Though Mr. Smith had promised to sit by her on the bus, there would be occasions like this one where circumstances dictated otherwise.

Now that she knew her chaperone desired her and was becoming more protective of her all the time,

Whitney decided to take advantage of the situation to make him jealous.

There was nothing like a little healthy competition to keep the fires burning until she had maneuvered him into a corner he couldn't get out of. Since she knew instinctively that he didn't care for Mr. Bowen, Whitney purposely took her seat next to Christine's old French teacher.

The gesture must have surprised Mr. Bowen whose face broke out in a welcoming smile. In fact he showed such enthusiasm to have her for a traveling companion, he appeared younger. For the first time she could understand how that enthusiasm impacted his adoring students and kept Christine one of his fans. Things couldn't have been more perfect if Whitney had orchestrated his reaction herself.

Throughout the drive to Fontainebleau, she gave him her exclusive attention. The occasional shuttered glance in Mr. Smith's direction told her he wasn't at all happy about the situation, at least not if his hardened facial features were any indicator of his mood. She didn't think he or Mr. Grimshaw had said a word to each other. The older man's head rested against the window, his eyes closed. It had been a long, uncomfortable flight.

Enjoying this more than anything she'd done in a long time, she continued to ply her seatmate with positive comments about his beautiful French accent and to praise his knowledge of French culture. As she hoped he would, Mr. Bowen preened under her compliments. She knew most teachers felt unappreciated. Any crumb thrown their way was considered manna from heaven.

Her plan seemed to be working. As soon as the bus pulled into the parking area outside the château, Mr. Smith called to her. She turned away from Mr. Bowen to face her chaperone who was already on his feet. Unsmiling gray eyes stared down at her, their expression enigmatic.

"Yes, Mr. Smith?"

"If you're ready to go—"

"Yes. Of course." She jumped to her feet. "I'm sorry. Mr. Bowen's stories about Fontainebleau were so fascinating, I lost track of the time." She turned to the other man, but not before she saw Mr. Smith's jaw harden. "Thanks for the history lesson, Mr. Bowen. I'm sure I'll get a lot more out of the tour now."

"Anytime, Whitney. We'll talk again."

"I'll look forward to it."

"After you," her chaperone reminded her in a quiet voice edged in steel. His possessiveness was showing.

A frisson chased across her skin. *Her plan was working.*

Without another word to her they got off the bus and waited for the boys to join them. Once everyone was assembled, they began the tour of the famous château where the Emperor Napoleon Bonapart had often resided. It was at Fontainebleau that he'd signed his abdication before going into exile on the island of Elba.

At any other time in her life Whitney would have loved this tour and thrilled to what she was learning. But she'd come for an entirely different purpose.

Little by little the tension between her and Mr. Smith was building. She'd provoked him for a reason, and now she feared she had awakened a sleeping tiger.

The showdown wouldn't be long in coming. That knowledge made it difficult to concentrate on anything else.

"The Emperor preferred this small bedroom," their guide explained as they toured the refurbished apartments originally built by Louis XVI. "If you'll notice, it has a mechanical desk and an iron bed. Not a room where he entertained the *femmes, n'est-ce pas?*"

His reference to the ladies brought a laugh from everyone except herself and Mr. Smith whose veiled gaze suddenly trapped hers at the mention of the bed.

As ridiculous as it was, heat scorched her cheeks. She looked away, pretending interest in the Diane garden outside the window, while inwardly she was confused by the jolt of desire that rocked her body.

What had started out as a game to entrap Mr. Smith appeared to be backfiring on her with devastating results.

"The furnishings reminded him of the ones he used in his military campaigns," the tour guide continued to explain. "He was a soldier at heart. Now follow me, please."

Relieved they could leave the warm, airless room, Whitney walked ahead of her chaperone along the François I gallery to the apartments formerly reserved for ceremonies. In the press of bodies she ended up standing next to Mr. Bowen.

"Fontainebleau is unique, but if you want to catch Napoleon's true essence, you must visit Malmaison, the small country house he built for Josephine when he divorced her."

"I don't recall that being on the itinerary."

"It's not, but I often take my students out there

when we have free time. After we've settled in at our hotel today, most of my group will want to catch a few hours sleep after having flown thousands of miles. That's why nothing is planned for the afternoon.

"However, I consider sleep a waste of time in this beautiful city. Those who wish can join me for the rest of the day. We'll be back in time for our dinner and cruise aboard the *bateau mouche*. Please feel free to join us, Whitney. It'll be well worth the trip. I'll pay the entrance fees. All you'll need is subway and bus fare."

A break from Mr. Smith might bring her some perspective which she desperately needed about now. The banked fires in his eyes moments ago warned her that her goal to seduce him had gotten out of hand. She needed to slow things down a little before she administered the *coup de grâce*.

Since most of the students would probably stay in their rooms until dinner, he'd never know if she left the hotel or not. Whitney no longer deemed it wise to arouse his jealousy.

"I'd really like to see Malmaison," she whispered back.

"I knew you were special." His smile came alive. "You have the true, inquiring mind. Students like you are a joy to teach."

"Thank you."

He had a generosity of spirit and chose the right words to build a student's self-esteem. Christine hadn't exaggerated. Her French teacher charmed you with his intelligence, his sense of fun and energy which hadn't been readily apparent from his physical appearance. She bet his family missed him when he came on these trips.

"I'll phone your room when I'm ready to go."

"I'll be ready."

After a typical veal lunch, everyone dispersed to their hotel rooms. Gerard made a call to his contact at Interpol requesting surveillance on Whitney while he caught up on some much needed sleep. He didn't worry about Jeff and Roger who were probably as exhausted as he was.

A deep sigh of relief escaped as he stretched out on top of the bed and phoned Roman before he passed out. He'd just come from the shower and had hitched a towel around his hips. After the heat of the day, the cool spray had felt good. So did the solitude.

Besides their own busload of students, there must have been a thousand tourists milling through the château at Fontainebleau until there hadn't been a breath of fresh air anywhere. In the crunch he'd seen Donald Bowen make a beeline for Whitney. The man was panting for her.

Obviously Bowen hadn't been happy that their conversation on the bus had been brought to a premature end. From a distance Gerard had watched the other man lie in wait for Whitney inside the château in order to corner her and resume dialogue.

Whatever he'd said to her, she hadn't chosen to share it with the group at lunch. When he'd helped carry her bag to her room, he had hoped she would confide in him privately, but she'd said nothing. Much to Jeff's and Roger's disappointment, she indicated she was going to take a nap.

Though puzzled by her reticence—because up to

this moment she had seemed so open about everything else—Gerard decided not to push her for the information. In time he would find out. The lowlife was starting to set her up. Gerard could feel it.

But the more he stared at the wall separating them, the more he struggled with the urge to walk next door and ask her to tell him what Bowen had been so anxious to discuss with her.

Of course there was one glaring reason why he couldn't do that.

She was alone in there because her friend Leslie had canceled too late for STI to arrange another roommate for her.

Gerard was trying his damnedest not to think of her standing under the spray, or lying on the bed fresh from the shower, her silvery-blond hair damp and sweet smelling...

"Oh, Lord." He groaned and turned on his stomach, willing certain images to leave his mind.

Without wasting another agonizing second, he reached for his cell phone and punched in the office number. This time Diana answered and told him to hold. Roman would pick up.

"Good morning, *Comrade.*"

"You don't have to sound so cheery," Gerard bit out with unaccustomed irritation. "Have a little pity. I haven't slept in thirty-six hours. Just tell me what I already know—that Whitney Lawrence is an innocent eighteen-year-old high school graduate who should never have crossed my path—and I'll be back in Salt Lake by tomorrow morning."

Silence greeted his ear.

"Roman?"

"First of all, I'll give you the information on Donald Bowen's wife. Her name is Mary Richins. According to Interpol, Bowen's story about his wife being born in Orem checks out. They have a five-year-old daughter, Tiffany. From all indications, his wife has no clue he's been leading a double life."

"And Whitney?"

After a slight pause, "Don't make return flight reservations yet."

At this juncture Gerard was on his feet, his heart pounding. "What are you saying?"

"There's no record of a Whitney Lawrence ever having attended Union High School, grade school, or middle school in Box Elder County. There are no Lawrence's in the area, period."

Gerard stopped pacing. *That meant—*

"That means your instincts are right on, as usual." Roman read Gerard's mind with alacrity. "I always said you're the best PI there is. We're running every check we know on her. Interpol is running their own. I'll have information on her by your time tomorrow morning at the latest. Give me a call before you leave for the tour of the Louvre."

"I will." Gerard knew it took time to gather that kind of intelligence, but he needed something he could grab on to now.

"At least you can stop worrying that you're a lecherous old man," Roman quipped, but Gerard was not amused.

The knowledge that Whitney was a devious woman, not an innocent teenager, brought him no joy.

Since the night at the library, she'd known he was attracted to her. Armed with that knowledge, she'd used him, come on to him, played up to him until she'd twisted him in knots. *And he'd fallen for every feminine trick.*

The hell of it was, despite what he'd just learned, he was *still* attracted. His emotions weren't going to automatically turn off no matter what his head was telling him.

Though he didn't know the connection between her and Bowen, or how her part worked in the scheme of things, Gerard was on to her. The rules of the game were about to change.

"Roman? I've got something to do that can't wait. Keep working on things from your end and I'll call you around noon your time. *I owe you.*"

Pulling on a clean pair of jeans, a lightweight knit shirt and shoes, he left his room and approached her door. After a couple of taps he called her name but she didn't answer. He rapped on the door a little harder. Still no response.

He went back to his room to phone her. After a dozen rings, he was convinced she'd gone out, even though she'd told the boys she intended to rest. It was a good thing he'd had her tailed.

Reaching for one of the tools he carried in a small case, he went back to her door. After a look around to make sure no one was in the hall, he played with the lock until he heard the click, then pushed the door open.

The three-star, economy hotel had postage-stamp-size rooms. At a glance, he could see she wasn't on the premises. He went inside and shut the door. Within a minute he'd cased the room and had gone through her luggage and toiletries. He didn't think anyone's eye color could be as beautiful as hers, so he looked for signs that she wore contact lenses. Nothing turned up.

The only thing the bathroom search revealed was her penchant for fairly expensive French perfume and fruit-flavored shampoo. She slept in knee-length nightgowns. There were no photographs around, no Walkman or cassettes, no wine or beer, no candy, no cigarettes or drugs. She was clean.

He'd been looking for her passport, but she must have taken it with her. Some of the labels in her clothes indicated she'd bought them in Salt Lake, but he found nothing that gave him a real clue as to her identity.

She'd brought a novel with her about Martha Stewart and the *Washington Post.* Not everyone's favorite reading material unless you wanted insight into the America of the past. A foreign agent might read it for a quick American history lesson.

The crossword puzzle he already knew about. She'd mastered the highest degree of difficulty without the use of a dictionary. Most people couldn't do it *with* one. But her intelligence was not in question here. Just her allegiance. *To which flag?*

He rubbed his chest absently. Did she always work with Donald Bowen, or was this a special assignment? Maybe Gerard had been wrong about the students being involved. Maybe the kids simply provided a smoke screen while the two masterminds worked on some unwitting teacher who had no idea he or she would end up assisting the enemy.

His thoughts darted back to Fran Ashton. With insight, he realized that Whitney—that was the name he would call her until he knew the truth—had done a good job of keeping him separated from the other teacher.

Not without your cooperation, Gerard had to remind himself. Maybe Fran was a pawn.

Too many possibilities were exploding inside him. But nothing mattered without the right information. Whitney's passport held the key.

Leaving everything as he found it, he let himself out and went back to his room to wait until she returned. Two hours later he knocked on her door before dinner. She opened it and almost jumped at the sight of Gerard standing there.

"Mr. Smith!"

"If you always open your door without asking who is on the other side, then you're in for some trouble you might not be able to handle. In future, call out first, otherwise I won't enjoy explaining to your grandmother that you were kidnapped or raped or something even worse."

"You're right," came her breathless answer. "I assumed it was Roger or Jeff."

"What makes you think you'd be any safer with them if they decided to have some fun with you and refused to take no for an answer?"

She blinked. "Your point is well taken."

"You look tired. Sometimes a nap makes the jet lag worse. I've learned that after an all night flight, it's still better to wait until the next night before going to bed."

She nodded. "You're preaching to the converted. Getting a little sleep has made me feel dreadful. Is it already time to go down to the bus?"

"Not quite yet. I'm here because I need your passport."

At the mention of the word, she blanched. Finally he'd broken through her incredible sangfroid.

"My passport?" Her voice sounded a little higher than normal. He was starting to enjoy this.

"That's right. I hated bothering you when I knew you were asleep. I tried calling you on the phone first, but you must have been dead to the world.

"There's been a security problem here at the hotel which is a fairly common occurrence during the day when people are out sight-seeing. Someone's camera was stolen.

"The police always check passports first. It's a routine formality. I'll bring yours right back so you won't have to deal with it."

Her lusterous violet eyes looked at him with such innocence, he had a hard time remembering she was the enemy. "I promised my grandmother I wouldn't let my passport out of my possession. Can the police come to my room instead?"

He'd been expecting any excuse except that one. She was a real pro.

"I don't see why that can't be arranged. I'll phone the front desk and explain the situation. Someone should be up here shortly."

"Thank you. Like I said before, I don't know what I'd do without you." She smiled shyly. "I'm looking forward to tonight. Dinner and dancing on the Seine. Do you dance, Hank?"

"Sometimes."

"Do the chaperones ever dance with their students?"

"Everyone joins in. The teachers, the driver, even the tour guide."

"Would you consider dancing with me?"

Gerard had to suppress another groan. Getting that close to her would not be a good idea no matter what game she was playing. "Of course. But I might not have the opportunity."

"Why do you say that?"

"I know a dozen boys at least who've made it clear they would like to get to know you better."

"But I'm not allowed to dance with them."

"That's right. You promised your grandmother. Won't she mind you dancing with a man old enough to be your father?"

She eyed him provocatively. "You *know* you don't look that old. I've heard what the girls have been saying about you behind your back. They're jealous you're my chaperone. There isn't one of them who wouldn't love to dance with you."

"Thank you, Whitney. That's the nicest thing anyone has said to me in a long time. I'll look forward to a dance with you. Now I need to go. Don't open your door until the police officer identifies himself. All right?"

"I'll never be as foolish again."

"Good. I'll see you down in the lobby in forty-five minutes."

"I'll be there."

He shut her door before returning to his room to make a call to the contact who'd been following her. He learned that she'd gone out to Malmaison with Mr. Bowen. Nothing untoward had happened. It had been a simple sight-seeing adventure. They'd talked to no one.

Gerard filed the information away, then explained the present situation. The agent said he would go to Whitney's room immediately, then report to Gerard.

While he waited, he phoned Yuri in New York to ask him a favor. By the time they'd hung up, Roman's brother had promised to be at the same hotel in Geneva when the tour arrived there.

During their conversation, they caught up on personal and family news, then devised a solid plan to check out Donald Bowen. It went without saying Gerard longed to see his good friend again.

No sooner had they said goodbye than he heard a knock on his door. The Interpol agent had disguised himself as a local gendarme. Gerard invited him inside.

"What did her passport say?"

"It's all here." Once he'd handed over the piece of paper, he left. Gerard scanned the man's notes.

"Surname, Lawrence. Given name, Whitney. Nationality, American. Date of birth, November 6, 1972."

She was twenty-six!

Here he'd been agonizing because he'd thought she was a teenager. She'd put him through hell!

"Sex, female. Place of birth, Utah, U.S.A. Date of Issue, April 29, 1998. Authority Passport Agency, San Francisco."

Except for finding out that she had lied to everyone about her age, especially to him, and that she had spent a couple of hours with Bowen, Gerard had learned nothing new. Roman would have to provide him the big answers. In the meantime, there was the rest of the evening to get through.

A dance to get through. Hell.

CHAPTER SIX

WHITNEY stood in the middle of her hotel room, still shaking from the close call.

If Mr. Smith hadn't agreed to let the gendarme come to her room to check her passport, her whole scheme to bring him down would have gone up in smoke. The gendarme wasn't concerned with her age, just that she was who she said she was.

No matter how well something was planned, you had to prepare for emergencies. Who would have guessed there would be a theft in the hotel her first day in Paris?

It had been a good wake-up call. She needed to step up her own agenda before something untoward occurred over which she might have no control.

That's why she'd pushed the idea of dancing with Mr. Smith. If she heated things up between them tonight, he would make his move faster.

Before leaving Salt Lake, she had imagined their confrontation coming toward the end of the tour. But because of the passport incident, she realized time wasn't on her side. The sooner he tried to take her to bed, the sooner she would have her evidence. But none of it could happen without her help.

Tonight she needed to dazzle him. Unfortunately she couldn't change her hairstyle without giving herself away. Not only did she have nothing in her teenage wardrobe to make a statement, she couldn't resort to makeup. The only thing left to do was flirt more openly. With less than a half hour before she had to be downstairs wearing her hidden microphone, there was no time to lose.

After spending a hot afternoon at Malmaison, the shower felt good. The only reason she'd decided to go with Mr. Bowen in the first place was so she could get away from Mr. Smith for a little while.

She certainly wouldn't have accompanied the other teacher if she hadn't thought some of his students would tag along. But at the last minute, everyone pleaded fatigue and no one wanted to leave the hotel.

Mr. Bowen had looked so disappointed, she didn't have the heart to disappointment him. As it turned out, she wasn't sorry for the experience. The home Napoleon had built for the wife he'd cast aside came as a charming surprise. With Mr. Bowen acting as her personal guide, French history came alive.

There was only one problem she could foresee. Being an avid Francophile, he obviously lived for these tours, even thrived on them. Several times as they'd been walking through Josephine's apartment, he'd mentioned taking Whitney on some other side trips throughout the tour because he knew how much she would appreciate them.

She'd been vague in her response, not wanting to hurt his feelings, but there was no way she would place herself in this kind of situation again. Even though he was married, she had the feeling he was lonely and craved companionship with someone who would enjoy these unique travel experiences.

Too bad his wife never came along, but she probably didn't share his love of the French language or its culture. It was little wonder he gravitated to his students, especially to someone like Whitney who'd been willing to listen to him. She supposed she had only herself to blame for unintentionally flattering him with her attention.

On the bus, when she'd impulsively decided to make Mr. Smith jealous, she'd turned to Mr. Bowen, never realizing how vulnerable he was.

It had been a bad idea, but not unsalvageable.

If she could bring Mr. Smith to his knees right away, she would be leaving the tour before she had to worry about coming up with reasons why she couldn't accompany Christine's former French teacher on any more out-of-the way sight-seeing trips.

In fact it was entirely possible that within a week, she'd be back at the law firm, content in the knowledge that she'd found her sister's lover and had forced him to deal with the son he'd fathered.

"May I have the last dance, *mademoiselle?*"

Whitney had been expecting the invitation all evening, but it was the wrong male voice addressing her in the balmy night air.

After finishing her dinner with Roger and Jeff who'd given up on her and had asked some other girls to dance, she had excused herself to wander over to the boat railing in the hope that Mr. Smith would follow her. That had been close to an hour ago.

Caught up in conversation with a couple of other teachers throughout their meal, she'd still felt his narrowed gaze on her from time to time. He knew exactly where she was at any given moment and could have asked her to dance at any time. Now it was too late.

The monuments of Paris, more beautifully lighted than a Christmas tree, provided a breathtaking backdrop. A band played *Petit Fleur* in the background. Everyone had been dancing for a long time. The setting was perfect for seduction.

But not with Mr. Bowen!

She turned around. "How nice of you to ask me, but I'm afraid I'm not feeling well. A slight case of dizziness. I think jet lag has finally caught up with me. We'll be docking in a moment and all I can think about is getting to bed."

"We did too much today. I feel responsible. How can I help?"

"Would you mind asking Mr. Smith to come over for a minute?"

"I'm right here, Whitney. What's wrong?"

He appeared as if out of thin air. In a dark blue dress shirt and chinos, he looked incredibly sexy and European. Her heart pounded outrageously. It wouldn't surprise her if both men could hear it.

Since boarding the *bateau mouche,* she'd hardly been able to take her eyes off her chaperone. The striking combination of tanned skin and dark blond hair, plus his tall, hard-muscled physique, had drawn her gaze over and over again. Many of the females on board were having the same problem.

"I'm afraid her jet lag has turned into something a little more serious. Since you were otherwise engaged, I was just about to arrange for a ride when we dock."

"I'm feeling under the weather myself. If you'll make sure Roger and Jeff get back on the bus safely with you, I'll accompany her in a taxi to the hotel.

Let's walk to the gate so we can be the first ones off
the boat, all right, Whitney?''

"Yes. Thank you, Mr. Smith.'' *Thank you.*

Without waiting for the other man's response, she
felt Mr. Smith's hand grasp her elbow and guide her
along the promenade deck toward the exit.

Though the man holding on to her was the evil one
of the piece, she was happy to get away from Mr.
Bowen. Another irony.

He'd been nothing but kind and solicitous the entire
trip, but he was starting to act possessive. The idea of
having to dance with him had sounded slightly repul-
sive to her.

Within five minutes, the boat pulled up to the dock
and they were ensconced in a taxi, away from the others.

"I'm sorry if you're not feeling well, Mr. Smith. Is
that why you didn't ask me to dance?''

In the confines of the back seat, her left leg lay
against his hard thigh. The heat generated between
them started a slow burn through the rest of her sen-
sitized body.

"I feel fine. The reason I didn't ask you to dance
was because you had already turned everyone else
down. To have accepted my invitation would have cre-
ated unnecessary gossip.''

"You're right. T-thank you for rescuing me.''

"It's obvious that Mr. Bowen has developed a slight
crush on you. I take it you don't reciprocate his feelings.''

"Hardly.''

"Then you shouldn't have been so affectionate with
him on the bus earlier.''

So he *had* noticed. She felt another stab of guilt for her impulsive mistake.

"All I tried to do was show him some attention so the others wouldn't think I had developed a crush on you. Except for you, no one else realizes I've made certain promises to my grandmother. I—I'm afraid my presence is just causing you a lot of trouble. It might be better if I make a reservation and fly back to Salt Lake tomorrow."

"Let me be the judge of that," he muttered. "Are you still feeling ill?"

"No. I made that up to discourage Mr. Bowen."

"I thought so. You still want to dance?"

"Do you?" she cried out softly, her body trembling in anticipation and fear of the moment when his arms would close around her.

"It's been a long time for me, but I think I can still remember a few moves. You can't be in Paris and not enjoy something of its nightlife, not even at your tender age."

She swallowed hard. "Do you know a nice place?"

"The *Pavillon* is around the corner from our hotel. It's an upper-class establishment, so you won't have to be concerned I'm taking you to an *endroit* your grandmother wouldn't approve of."

The more time she spent in his company, the more Whitney wished he weren't the man who had seduced her sister. So far he'd been the perfect chaperone who'd never once crossed the invisible lines of decency. He came off as a pretty perfect man!

Except for tonight.

Tonight, instead of taking her directly to the hotel, he was going to make her wish come true and dance with her. Strictly speaking, he shouldn't be doing this, at least not with one of his female students.

"If you don't feel right about this, Whitney, just say the word and I'll have the chauffeur drive us to the hotel."

"I'm quiet because I've been thinking how wonderful you are to be this nice to me."

"You're easy to be nice to."

"Am I dressed all right to go there?"

His head swiveled around. In the semidarkness she felt his penetrating gaze. "Your skirt and blouse look lovely."

He was a master of understatement, yet the sexual tension emanating from him seemed explosive.

Her mouth went dry. "You don't dress like the other teachers."

"Don't you approve?" His voice grated.

"I meant it as a compliment."

"Then I'll take it as one."

Whitney was desperately trying to imagine her sister having this kind of conversation with him. Even now Christine was a young nineteen. Somehow Whitney couldn't see either of them together on an intellectual or emotional level, and certainly not in the throes of great passion.

Because you don't want to see?

"We've arrived."

He levered himself from the seat, then helped her out. As in the library auditorium last week, he urged her forward with his hand on the back of her waist. Her body hadn't forgotten his touch and seemed almost embarrassingly eager for the contact.

The crowded dance bar featured a live band that

played ballades rather than rock. She looked around at the older, well-dressed crowd, excited and nervous to be here with him.

They were shown to a table where he ordered a glass of white wine for both them. "To help us sleep later," was all he said by way of explanation.

Wondering if he meant that before the night was over they would end up in bed together, she was afraid to look at him just then.

This is what you wanted, Whitney. Why the hesitation?

Suddenly she felt a strong male hand grasp hers and pull her up from the chair. She lifted her stunned gaze to his.

"You wanted to dance? Let's not waste any time."

Slowly he drew her toward him. She went into his arms as if it were the most natural thing in the world.

Within seconds she felt the length of his hard male body, from his shoes to his cheek with its trace of five o'clock shadow.

Dear God. A fire enveloped her that went on forever, yet never consumed.

Their bodies were a perfect fit. As she looped her arms around his neck, his hands moved down her back with growing urgency, possessive and exploring. The sensation left her breathless.

Whitney had known physical desire before. But this cataclysm of excitement went beyond the bounds of anything she'd ever experienced because she could sense his overpowering desire for her, too.

With every movement, their bodies throbbed with wanting. It was agony because they were on a dance floor, fully clothed, in sight of other people. Their closeness wasn't enough. They both wanted and needed much more.

So many feelings were erupting, vying for supremecy, she was in danger of forgetting why she'd come on the tour. For a few minutes, she'd forgotten that this man was wicked, that he had behaved in exactly the same manner with Christine.

This might be a new and sacred experience for Whitney, but she was simply another teenage conquest to this flawed teacher who exploited younger women for pleasure.

What greater proof did she need than to remember that a little over a year ago, he'd seduced her sister with just as much passion as he was showing Whitney right now?

She'd wanted to nail the person who'd caused her sister such grief. Tonight was her chance! He was barely holding on to his control as it was. All she needed to do was one more thing, and she could name the place and minute of his demise.

"Hank?" she whispered, brushing her lips against the cords of his neck while her breath came in shallow pants. "I don't think I'll be able to stand it if you don't kiss me. I'm aching for you."

"You must be reading my mind," he murmured into her hair. "Let's get out of here."

His hand slid to hers. He drew her to the table where he placed a number of large bills next to their untouched drinks, then he led her out of the bar to a waiting taxi.

Once inside, he pulled her onto his lap with shocking swiftness. She heard him say something to the chauffeur, then he caught her face between his hands.

"I know you're only eighteen, Whitney, but so help me, I want you, and I know you want me. If it's a crime, then so be it."

He lowered his head and covered her mouth with his own, urging her lips apart with a refined savagery that thrilled every inch of her being, yet frightened her.

On fire for him, she could deny him nothing.

For the next little while their mouths fused in passion. The more they attempted to satisfy the clamoring needs of their bodies, the more they hungered. They were still giving each other kiss for kiss when the taxi came to an unexpected halt.

"Why have we stopped so soon?" she moaned against lips that continued to devour hers. "Where are we?"

"In an alley at the rear of our hotel. You're going to use the back entrance and go in first. I'll follow in a few minutes and come to your room."

Good. That would give her enough time to gather her wits before she accomplished what she'd been planning for the last few months.

"I don't want to leave you. I'm afraid you'll do the honorable thing and decide to stay away from me."

He bit out an unintelligible epithet. "I haven't felt honorable about you since the first moment I laid eyes on you." There was a sharp intake of breath. "If you think I'd let you go now, then you don't know anything about men. Trust me, Whitney. This night is just beginning."

Oh, I do trust you. Now hear me. Before this night

is over you're going to receive the reward you deserve.

Gerard watched her hurry inside the back door of the hotel, her hair a glorious banner of gilt.

He knew the driver was waiting for him to get out of the taxi, but he couldn't move. Not yet. Whitney Lawrence had done things to him. Amazing things.

He'd known desire before. Certainly it had been there for his wife. But he couldn't recall ever wanting a woman so much in his life. Not even with Simone had he experienced this explosion of need.

The urge to make love to Whitney on that dance floor almost overcame his reason.

He'd once met a Gypsy outside Budapest who had tried to make him buy a potion that was supposed to create insatiable needs and bring new excitement to his lovemaking. One taste of it and he would crave more and more.

Gerard had scoffed at the absurd notion. True love between a man and a woman generated that kind of passion on its own.

So how did he account for this unquenchable fire burning him alive when the female in question was working with a foreign agent wanted by Interpol for espionage crimes?

The sweet taste of Whitney was still fresh on his lips. He feared her effect on him was like that mythical potion. It didn't seem to matter that she was playing a dangerous game. The craving for her was growing stronger.

"Monsieur?" The driver wanted his money. Naturally he did.

Gerard handed him a bill and got out of the taxi. On his way up the back stairs of the hotel, just the thought of Whitney and the way she made him feel produced a surge of adrenaline that couldn't possibly be healthy.

His senses seemed to be more acute. Her mere presence heightened his excitement to be alive, to be a man. He hadn't been to sleep in forty-eight hours, yet he'd never been more fully awake.

He knew that when he returned to his room, he would end up in hers and there didn't seem to be anything he could do about it.

In the past, he'd never made love to a woman unless they'd shared a meaningful relationship first. Even then, there had only been a few relationships apart from his marriage. That was the code he'd always lived by.

So why now was he about to break his own rule with a woman he would probably end up sending to prison?

Coming from the other end of the hall, he reached her door first. Beyond the point of no return, he tapped lightly.

She opened it so fast it took his breath away. Her gorgeous face and figure took *his* breath away.

"Tell me it's too late and I won't come in." He had to say it to satisfy the wretched voice that used to be his conscience. Tomorrow he would face the harsh reality of her double life.

Tonight the edges were blurred, marring his ability to think. All roads led to her. That was all he knew. Until morning he would pretend she was the innocent eighteen-year-old he'd fallen in love with.

Those violet eyes never wavered. "I was terrified you wouldn't come. What took you so long?"

The only escape hole filled over his head. He shut the door and reached for her.

For a long time they clung to each other, relishing the differences between man and woman as they feasted on each other's mouths, unable to get enough.

Without an audience they had no inhibitions and all the time in the world to touch and be touched. Her warmth and fragrance intoxicated him.

He didn't remember gravitating to the bed. The sound of her high heels falling to the floor gave the only clue that he'd carried her the short distance. It was too small for them, but somehow they fit anyway.

After burying his face in her hair so he could revel in its silkiness, he lifted his head and stared into her darkly fringed eyes. In the dim light of the dresser lamp they glowed like precious gemstones, shot with blue and lavender fire.

The shape of her mouth lured him to trace it with his index finger. "I want you, Whitney, but you already know that. Obviously I haven't let your young age stand in the way of what I desire. That's wrong of me, I know.

"But when two people are as physically attuned as we are and have been since the meeting in Salt Lake, it seems equally wrong to deny the intensity of those feelings, or to hope they'll go away.

"I only know of one method to cure the ache we're both experiencing, at least for tonight. Whether you believe me or not, I've never wanted any woman so much before."

"Not even your wife?" came the tremulous question.

"Not even my wife," he whispered, having already admitted that truth to himself. Simone was part of the past, when he had been a very young man. *I'm a grown man now. What I feel with you can't be described or compared to any other experience.*

"Are you divorced, or did she die?"

With that question, she gave herself away, jerking him back to ugly reality.

Whitney Lawrence was on a quest for information. What exactly did she want to know? Had Bowen become suspicious of Gerard and told her to find out what she could? Was this part of the plan they'd hatched out at Malmaison?

Until Gerard heard from Roman and knew Whitney's true agenda, it would be wisest to vacate her bed and call it a night, difficult as that was going to be to do.

"I don't blame you for asking that question." He kissed her long and hungrily. "Naturally you want to know everything there is to know about me before we make love for the first time. I agree there should be no secrets between us.

"Though I don't feel gentlemanly, I'm going to do the gentlemanly thing and slow things down a little. You're so young and vulnerable, I have no right to touch you, but I can't seem to help myself," he said in a husky voice. "I don't want to make any mistakes with you. I need you to be very sure this is what you want."

"But I *do* wa—"

"Trust me, Whitney." He quieted her protest with

another deeply satisfying kiss. He would never be able to get enough of her. "We have plenty of time and opportunity to learn all the private, intimate things there are to know about each other. Our tour has only just begun.

"When we reach Switzerland, there are places I want to take you where we can be totally private and make love to our hearts content. Right now isn't the time. Besides, you're almost ready to pass out on me."

Exhaustion had only enhanced her beauty. Her eyes were glazed by passion. That part she couldn't hide or fake. The chemistry between them was so powerful, if he didn't remove himself from her arms in the next minute, he wouldn't be going anywhere. Such a mistake could jeopardize everything.

She studied his features longingly. At the same time her hands molded his shoulders, driving him insane with needs he could barely control. "After tonight it will be hard to pretend we're just student and teacher in front of the others," she whispered.

"You don't know the half of it. Whitney—" He sucked in his breath. "For the rest of the tour I'm going to be seen spending a little more time with the boys. Rest assured it's a ploy to protect you from further gossip. Do you understand?"

"I'll understand as long as you promise we're going to be together in Switzerland. *Really* together."

"I swear it," he vowed before his mouth closed over hers one more time. A few minutes later he buried his face against her throat to kiss the warm, scented hollow, then he stole away.

With a sense of dread he returned to his own claustrophobic hotel room and its empty bed.

CHAPTER SEVEN

WHITNEY undressed quickly and got ready for bed. Though she was dead on her feet, she stared into the darkness long after he'd gone, torn apart by conflicting emotions.

Tonight she'd come close to exposing him. In fact she could have forced the issue. But when he suggested they take things slow and easy, she decided her revenge would be all the sweeter if she waited until he felt the timing was right. Then the setting for the crime would be *his* creation.

The more she thought about it, the more she realized the seduction scene should not take place in *her* hotel room where she could be blamed for enticing him. Under the law, that kind of setup was known as entrapment.

No. She needed the kind of proof that would place the blame wholly on his shoulders.

His shoulders. His mouth. That magnificent male body...

Whitney groaned out loud because her body was still reacting to the passion he had aroused. The scent of the soap he used still clung to her skin. She explored her swollen lips with a sense of wonder.

Did Christine lie awake nights haunted by the same soul-destroying memories?

Of course she did!

The two of them had made love twice. Christine

110

had memories Whitney could only imagine. Christine had borne his son who would probably grow up to be every bit as attractive as his father.

Before Whitney succumbed to sleep, she found herself wondering how many paternity suits could be brought against him if anyone took the trouble to find out? How many naive teenage girls had known rapture in his arms?

When Gerard first heard a phone ring, he thought he was dreaming and covered his head with his pillow. The ringing started again. On about the tenth ring, he realized it was his cell phone, not the hotel's. *Roman!*

He grabbed for it and said hello.

"Before you yell at me for disturbing the dead, I thought you ought to hear this. It might make you feel a little better."

Nothing could make him feel better. "I assume we're talking about Whitney Lawrence. I don't know if I can handle any news about her right now."

"Not even if we don't think she has any connection with Bowen?"

Gerard flung off the covers and sat up, his heart thudding. "Say that again?"

"She's a corporate attorney with Sharp and Rowe law firm in Salt Lake."

Whitney Lawrence was an attorney? Gerard raked a hand through his hair. Sharp and Rowe was one of the more well-established, prestigious firms located in the Kennecott Building.

"Still feel you can't handle any more news?"

Gerard's emotions were in chaos. "*Lord,* Roman!"

"Amen. She recently passed the Utah bar with high

marks. It will interest you to know she graduated from the University of Utah Law School *magna cum laude*."

That explained her crossword puzzle and choice of reading material.

"She was born and raised in Salt Lake, attended East Valley High School, graduated with honors, four point average all four years. Was a pianist for the orchestra and choir, won the Sterling Scholar Award in Business and was captain of the East Valley ski team that brought home the coveted Peruvian Trophy all four years."

That meant she'd spent a lot of time training for her ski races in Alta, Gerard's backyard. Those would have been the years he'd been working for Interpol in Europe.

"There's more. In college, she did a summer internship in Senator Pike's office in Washington, D.C., and is serving on the Governor's Board for the 2002 Olympics."

The information was coming faster than Gerard could absorb.

"She's never been married. As far as we can tell, there's no man currently in her life. Except you, of course," Roman added adroitly. "She lives alone in the Millcreek Road apartment complex."

Gerard blinked. He passed that apartment on his way to the office every morning.

"She owns a 1997 Jeep Wrangler and is still paying off a student loan. Her father died years ago and her mother remarried a Thomas Mason. She has an unmarried half sister, Christine, and a nephew named Greg.

"Before now she has never traveled outside the U.S. except for two trips to Acapulco and Matzatlan which only required a visa. We don't place her in any area or time frame that would coincide with Donald Bowen's known movements."

After a long silence Gerard blurted, *"What in the hell is she doing on this trip posing as a teenager?"*

"That's for you to find out, *Comrade*. Perhaps now I can wish you happy hunting. Go back to sleep. We'll talk later."

"I forgive you for the phone call," Gerard muttered.

"I thought you would." There was a click.

He stood there with the phone still clutched in his hand. Whitney Lawrence had an agenda all right, but he'd thought that in spite of it, the chemistry between them had been real and spontaneous.

After hearing of her background and accomplishments, he realized she had the brains and the capacity to carry off any charade as long as it furthered her objectives.

Could a woman fake the response she'd shown him tonight? Had she decided to use him for her own purposes because he was on the spot and available?

Upon introspection he found the idea of either of those questions being answered with a yes untenable.

As to whether or not Whitney would go so far as to finish what they'd started earlier tonight, he guessed he would find out when they got to Switzerland. In the meantime, maybe he ought to do the job he was being paid for and nail Bowen.

Needing something to lower his temperature, he headed for another cold shower.

* * *

"Hey, Whitney? Come with us this afternoon."

The tour group had finished lunch after coming back from the Louvre and had split up for the rest of the day. Some had gone with their teachers to the Gare D'Orsay Museum. Others from Mr. Grimshaw's group had befriended Whitney and wanted her to go with them to the Pompidou Center.

Much as Whitney would have loved to see some of the Impressionist paintings, she knew Mr. Smith was headed there with Jeff and Roger. He had said he was going to spend the bulk of his time with them. After the intimacy they'd shared last night, she needed to stay away and sort out her feelings, which were growing more confused.

If she ended up alone with him again, she was afraid she wouldn't have the strength to deny him. The desire for that closeness was so powerful, she no longer trusted herself with him.

In fact today might be a good day to isolate herself from everyone.

As unobtrusively as possible, she approached him at one of the tables of the sidewalk café. "Mr. Smith?"

At the sound of her voice his head turned in her direction, casting her an enigmatic regard. But she knew he was remembering last night. They'd kissed each other senseless and she still hadn't recovered. "What is it, Whitney?"

His nearness made it hard to think. "I'm going to stay at the hotel this afternoon. I want to call my grandmother and write a few postcards to friends."

"Thanks for telling me. If you decide not to join us

after dinner for the opera, then don't forget we leave early in the morning for Versailles.''

Neither of the boys hearing that response would think anything was going on between her and their chaperone.

"I won't.'' She smiled at the guys. "Have a good time.''

Much later in the day, after she'd called her family and had chatted with John Warren, she gave a surreptitious glance around the lobby hoping none of the group were still here, then left the hotel to visit the place housing Rodin's works. She'd studied the famous sculptor in college, hoping one day to see his statues in person.

Within ten minutes a taxi had deposited her near the museum where she had her first glimpse of *The Thinker*. The sight of the famous masterpiece should have thrilled her, but her involvement with Mr. Smith consumed her thoughts, robbing her of the full pleasure she should be feeling at this rare opportunity. Without him standing next to her, the excitement had gone out of the day. *I miss him.*

Disturbed by this knowledge, she moved inside to view *The Shades* and *The Cathedral*, two acclaimed works. As she stood there marveling over them, her eye caught sight of a marble statue farther away. She started toward it, then realized she was staring at *The Kiss*.

The way the man was kissing the woman took her breath. Rodin had captured the two lovers' emotions in the stone so they appeared lifelike.

After last night she shouldn't be looking at anything this intimately beautiful. It seemed to capture the essence of what she'd felt with Mr. Smith. *What she couldn't forget...*

"This is my favorite piece, too. You're a true lover of the arts, aren't you, Whitney? Your French teacher prepared you well for this tour."

Mr. Bowen's voice. She'd thought he'd gone with his students, but there were no set rules. The teachers covered for one another to allow flexibility.

His showing up here was obviously a coincidence. She just wished she could have spent this afternoon alone, and preferred to be standing in front of any other statue than Rodin's most erotic work.

"Hello, Mr. Bowen. I thought you would be at the Pompidou."

He gave her a half smile, cocking his head. "Once is enough. When I'm in Paris I always visit certain treasured spots, this being one of them. Unfortunately the museum is closing, and I need to get back to my students. Shall we share a taxi to the hotel so we won't be late?"

Whitney glanced at her watch, surprised to discover it was five o'clock. Last night's memories had caused her to lose track of the time.

Much as she didn't want to accompany him, she had little choice. He had no idea she wasn't a student. Naturally he would expect her to go along with his suggestion since they were both returning to the same place anyway.

"Thank you, Mr. Bowen."

She followed him out of the gallery where he signaled a taxi. After giving the driver instructions, he settled back and turned to her with a smile.

"Before we reach the hotel, we're going to stop at

a special gift shop where they import puppets. I always order something to take home to my daughter. Perhaps there will be an item you would like to buy as a souvenir?''

A puppet sounded too old a gift for her nephew, but she couldn't go home empty-handed. Her thoughts darted back to a previous trip to Acapulco where panhandlers had tried to sell her a string puppet as she lay sunbathing on the beach.

If she could find one of those, she could always tell Christine to hang it on the wall till Greg grew older. It would be the perfect gift to back up the lie that Whitney had gone to Mexico on vacation.

More than ever she didn't want the family to know where she'd really been.

"Thanks. Maybe I will."

Before long they pulled up in front of the shop. Mr. Bowen instructed the chauffeur to wait.

The proprietor greeted Christine's French teacher like an old friend. Whitney wandered around fascinated by the varieties of puppets.

It didn't take her long to spot a little Mexican boy in a sombrero and white pants whose parts moved by strings. While the owner wrapped it up for her, Mr. Bowen put in an order for Esmerelda from the Hunchback of Notre Dame series. The other man promised that the hand puppet would be ready for pick-up when the tour came back to Paris for the flight home.

With that accomplished, they left the shop and climbed in the taxi. During the short trip to the hotel Mr. Bowen explained that the Esmerelda puppet would complete his daughter's Victor Hugo collection.

Anxious to get back before Mr. Smith discovered she'd been out, she only half listened to the other man's explanation. Once they arrived at the hotel, she excused herself to race up to her room where she planned to stay put for the rest of the evening.

Tomorrow night they would be sleeping in Dijon, the next night, Geneva. The Swiss portion of the tour was about to begin. A tremor of excitement passed through her body just imagining being alone with him again. She knew it was the wrong reaction for a woman who was planning his downfall, but she could no longer control her emotions where he was concerned.

Around eight-thirty the phone rang, making her jump. She'd been trying to get absorbed in her book but it was impossible to concentrate. Since Mr. Smith had gone to the opera with the boys, she couldn't imagine who it would be. Hesitantly she reached for the receiver and said hello.

"Whitney?"

At the sound of her chaperone's deep male voice her mouth went dry and her heart began to palpitate out of rhythm. She slid off the bed and stood up.

"Yes?"

"Did I wake you?"

"No."

You should have said yes, Whitney. You have no willpower at all around him.

"Roger isn't feeling well so we came back from the opera early. Though he would never admit it, I think he's suffering culture shock and has a touch of homesickness on top of it. If you were to take him a Coke and talk to him and Jeff for a little while, I think his spirits would improve. I'll be right next door, so you won't have to worry about being alone with them for more than a few minutes.''

Insane as it was, she felt a momentary pang of disappointment at the reason for his call, then scoffed at herself.

What were you waiting for? Were you hoping he would ask if he could join you in your room? Are you out of your mind?

Though Mr. Smith was a womanizer of young women, she felt a grudging respect for his concern over Roger. Whitney had experienced a bout of homesickness when she'd first gone to Washington, D.C., to work. It was an awful feeling and she could commiserate with Roger's condition.

''I'll get a bunch of drinks from downstairs and then go to their room.''

''Thank you. Don't let on that you know anything, or that this was my suggestion.'' After a slight pause, ''I know you're on a tight budget so I'll reimburse you later tonight.''

Later tonight?

She swallowed hard. It sounded like he'd changed his mind about waiting until they reached Switzerland to be alone together. Deep inside she knew he wanted her as much as she wanted him.

''Okay.''

Still dressed in jeans, blouse and loafers, all she had to do was attach the microrecorder to the inside collar of her blouse and she was ready to leave the room.

When Gerard saw her blond head disappear down the stairs, he broke into her room, curious to know what she'd bought in the shop on the way home from the museum. Bowen, who'd been a few steps behind her, had exited the store empty-handed.

With Mr. Hart's help, Gerard had been freed from the boys so he could tail Donald Bowen's movements after lunch. It came as no surprise to discover the other man had followed Whitney out of the hotel to the museum.

A quick search of her room produced the brown sack sitting on the dresser with the words 'Au Souk Maroc' printed on the paper. A souk was a North African market.

Inside he found a Mexican puppet of all things.

A deep crease furrowed his brow as he put the sack down and returned to his own room.

Why would she purchase such a souvenir when she was in *France?* At the least he would have expected something of Moroccan make. Before the night was out, he intended to have an answer to that question.

Gerard had purposely planned an evening at the opera so the boys would moan and want to come back to the hotel early.

He'd lied to Whitney about Roger's homesickness, but she would never know. It had been a perfect ploy to get her away from her room. Now he needed a different ruse to be alone with her again.

He left his room and tapped on the boys' door.

Jeff opened it a crack, then looked nervous when he discovered who was on the other side.

"Hi, Hank."

"Hi, Jeff. What's going on?"

"Nothing much."

Gerard chuckled inwardly. "I could hear your

laughter clear down the hall. What girl have you got in there with you?''

A guilty expression washed over the teen's face. ''Whitney came by with some Cokes for us. That's all. I swear it!''

''I believe you, but you know the rules about no girls in your room.''

''Hey—'' he said in a hushed tone. ''This is our first chance to be alone with her. You know what I mean.''

''Unfortunately I *do*.''

Jeff's expression became mutinous. ''We just want to get to know her a little better. Is that a crime? We're all eighteen. At home we—''

''That's the problem, Jeff,'' he interrupted the younger man. ''You're not home. You're on a tour and I'm responsible for all of you.''

''Ah, come on, Hank. It's barely ten o'clock, and we're in Paris. *Jeez*.''

Once upon a time Gerard had been Jeff's age and knew exactly how he felt.

''Sorry. Rules are rules.''

He pushed the door open a little farther. At a glance he noticed Whitney on a chair facing Roger who sat barefoot on one of the beds, his face wreathed in a smile. But it faded when he saw Gerard come in the room. All at once he was on his feet.

''Hi, Hank. Whitney just dropped in for a minute.''

''So I see.''

Both teens had a serious crush on her. No one knew how that felt better than Gerard. His mind and body remembered the way she'd clung to him the night before. Over and over again he relived the explosion of excitement her mouth generated with every hungry kiss.

She's lit a fire in you, Roche.

The exultation he felt because it appeared she wasn't working with Donald Bowen made it burn that much hotter. He might not have all the answers where she was concerned, but right now nothing seemed more important than getting tangled in her arms again.

"If you've all finished your drinks, then I suggest everyone turn in. We have to be down in the lobby for breakfast by six a.m. It's going to be a long day tomorrow."

Whitney got out of her chair. "I've had a lot of fun, guys. We'll have to do it again."

"Yeah," they both said in unison, disappointment dripping from their response.

Gerard patted both students on the shoulders. *"Bon soir, mes amis. Dormez bien."*

Repressing a smile, he followed Whitney from the room and shut the door behind him. No one else was in the hall.

It was all he could do not to slide his hands around the womanly thrust of her hips and draw her against him.

"I think your presence helped Roger feel a good deal better."

"Roger didn't act homesick in front of me."

Naturally she'd noticed.

"Of course not. He has his pride. At this point he's upset with me for breaking things up, which means your visit distracted him enough to get his mind off himself for a little while. Come in my room and I'll pay you back for the drinks."

He opened his door and waited for her to pass in front of him. Though she hesitated, he knew in his gut she wanted to be with him. Their kind of chemistry was rare. It ran marrow deep.

He noticed her look around to see if they were alone before she moved inside. Adrenaline charged his body.

When the click of the door sounded she turned to him, her cheeks slightly flushed. For the first time since they'd met, he could swear she was nervous. Her reaction intrigued him.

He reached for his wallet on the dresser and pulled out twenty francs.

"You don't need to pay me back, Mr. Smith. I didn't mind buying them a couple of Cokes."

"It's the least I can do considering how hard you worked to earn the money to come on this trip." *No one worked harder or longer hours than a new attorney in a corporate law firm.*

He moved closer, extending the French notes once more. When she still refused to take them, he reached for her hand and folded the bills in her palm. "I'm the chaperone, and I asked you to do me a personal favor. The welfare of my students has to be my first priority. *Yours* ranks at the top, Whitney, and we both know why."

"You mean because of the promise to my grandmother."

"I mean because twice now, you've told me you were going to stay in your room instead of going out with the others. Yet twice you've left the hotel without informing me of your plans."

Her eyes had widened. *"Twice?"*

"Yesterday you were spotted with Mr. Bowen on the subway from Neuilly. Today a couple of students taking a bus tour of Paris happened to mention seeing you and Mr. Bowen coming out of a building in a seedier part of the city."

Taking advantage of her astonishment, he grasped her upper arms. The feel of her warm, scented flesh tantalized him. He could well imagine Bowen's plans for her. The thought of that swine's hands on her body…

"Do you have any conception of the dangerous game you're playing?" His voice grated. Before he realized it, he'd shaken her. Though he could see the hint of alarm in her eyes, he refused to let up until he'd wrung a confession from her.

"Don't you know he's a married man with a child? If you've been trying to make me jealous, then you've done a good job, *cherie.* I thought you and I shared something special," he whispered against the vulnerable hollow of her throat. A throbbing pulse just beneath the skin revealed her heightened excitement.

"We do!" she exclaimed in a breathless voice. "I admit I played up to him on the bus to make you jealous, but that was the only time."

Her answer sounded like the truth. Obeying an age-old urge, Gerard pulled her into his body and pressed a hard, swift kiss to her mouth. "You knew how much I wanted you on the flight over. The attention you paid Mr. Bowen not only wasn't necessary, I'm afraid you played right into his hands."

He felt her stiffen. "What do you mean?"

"Hasn't it occurred to you that a man who leaves his wife and family every year to come on a student tour is looking for female company? Who better than some young, beautiful creature like yourself? Someone who admires him and feeds his ego?

"At least *I,* for all my sins, am free to love whom I will, even if you are young enough to be my daughter."

A long silence ensued. Something profound seemed to be going on inside of her. She gave him a soul-searching glance, almost as if she'd never seen him before.

"You really love me?" She sounded incredulous.

"I think you know I do. But I wager Mr. Bowen told you the same thing when he made love to you yesterday."

Her gently rounded chin lifted a trifle. "Yesterday I thought it would be better if you and I weren't seen together so much. So when Mr. Bowen announced he was taking any students who wanted to go out to Malmaison, I decided to join his group."

"And too late you found out you were his only student," he inserted in an ironic tone.

"Yes."

His brows drew together. "That might explain yesterday, but what about today? Tell me— did he take you to a hotel, or does he have an apartment?"

A tremor rocked her body he could feel to his insides. What had he said to produce such a violent reaction?

"Neither one," she confessed at last. "You have to believe I've never let him touch me or be alone with me like this." Her earnestness was very compelling, but he needed more answers.

"I'm afraid you wouldn't convince Roger or Jeff."

Kneading her shoulders because he couldn't seem to keep his hands off her, he said, "As far back as Salt Lake they saw and heard how disappointed you were when the woman from STI put you in my group instead of his."

"That's because a friend of mine had recommended traveling with Mr. Bowen," she argued. "That was before I met *you,* Hank!"

"I might believe you if I hadn't witnessed the two of you making secret arrangements to be together while we toured the château at Fontainebleau.

"Later, aboard the boat, the man was devouring you with his eyes for all the world to see. Jeff even commented to Roger that it looked like Mr. Bowen had the hots for you. *His* words...not mine."

You just told another lie, Roche, but it's all necessary until you find out what went on when she was alone with Bowen. "Last night I actually thought you wanted rescuing."

"I did! I was waiting for you to ask me to dance."

"If that's true, then how come today I discovered that you not only had lied to me about intending to stay in your hotel room—you slipped out and spent an entire afternoon with *him.*"

Gerard's hands tightened on her shoulders. "You little fool, Whitney. You disappeared with a virtual stranger in a city that swallows people alive. He could have taken you anywhere, manipulated you into doing anything he wanted because of his position of power over you. There would have been no one to help you."

Her eyes clouded to an intense purple, as if she'd never entertained the thought before. But that couldn't possibly be, because she was a grown, savvy woman. One, furthermore, who had a background in the law.

"For a long time I did stay in my room," she began. "At the last minute I decided to go to the museum. Toward closing time he appeared. Naturally I assumed it was a coincidence. He asked me if I'd like to share a taxi back to the hotel. Since I would have gotten one anyway, I saw no reason not to join him."

Gerard took a steadying breath. "Even if that were true, how come you ended up in another part of town with him? The area where the students spotted you wasn't anywhere near the museum."

"He stopped by a shop to order a present for his daughter," she murmured, sounding very far away. "Since I wanted to buy a gift for my nephew, I went in with him."

"Then the students saw you coming out of a store?"

"Yes."

The lovely face he cradled in his hands had lost some of its color. What was going on inside of her?

"I want to believe you, but twice you've lied to me. How do I know you're not lying to me now? Whitney—" His gaze bore into hers. "Don't you know you've come to mean everything to me?"

Unable to help himself, he brushed his lips against hers. To his surprise, hers were trembling ever so slightly. "If anything were to happen to you, how do you suppose I would feel?"

Even to his own ears, his voice sounded husky. That was because he realized he'd spoken the truth. In the brief time he'd known her, she'd become more important to him than he dared admit.

CHAPTER EIGHT

As PURE revelation flowed through her, Whitney weaved and would have fallen if Mr. Smith hadn't been holding on to her.

Mr. Bowen was the father of Christine's baby, not Mr. Smith!

There was no doubt in Whitney's mind. Her first instincts that her sister had fallen in love with her French teacher of three years had been right all along. Everything fit.

He was married, he had a daughter, he always bought her a toy and he singled out the female student who showed all the signs of hero worship. Once he'd determined which student to exploit, he went to work on her...

But if that were true, then it meant Whitney had been seducing the *wrong man!*

Slowly she eased herself out of Mr. Smith's arms and backed away from him. Since the night in the Salt Lake library when she'd first laid eyes on him, his devastating masculine appeal had caused her to make the instant decision that *he* was the teacher who had compromised her sister.

Now that she knew differently, what did it say about Mr. Smith? How many years had he been pulling the same stunts as Mr. Bowen?

Were all the men on this tour immoral?

Wasn't there one man among them who could be

trusted with a bunch of silly high school girls who didn't have a clue what their male chaperones were up to?

"What's wrong, Whitney? You look ill." The concern in his eyes and voice seemed real enough. He was a master con artist, a monster disguised in breathtaking male form.

Fortunately she was on to Hank.

Before this tour was over, she would have enough documented evidence on both men to go to the district attorney with her findings.

Putting on the greatest acting performance of her life, she looked at him through misty eyes. "I *feel* ill because you don't believe me," she purposely put a wobble in her voice. "You see, I've fallen in love with you, too, Hank."

She made fists at her sides to convince him of her agony. "I—I can't bear it that you would think I would lie to you, let alone be interested in Mr. Bowen. If you want proof, I think I still have the ticket stub from the museum."

After rummaging in her pocket, she found it. "Yes—here it is. I can also show you the toy I bought for my nephew." She extended the half ticket to him but he didn't take it. Instead, he let out a deep sigh, raking his hands through his dark blond hair.

"Put it away, Whitney. I believe you. I guess I overreacted because I'm jealous of the time you've spent with Mr. Bowen. The fact of the matter is, you make me feel young again. Younger men tend to love rather possessively. That's how I feel about you. Very territorial."

"You do?" She feigned an ingenuous tone. He was so good at what he did, it was frightening.

He nodded. "I'm afraid I've gotten to the point where I want your exclusive attention."

"But you told me you were going to give Roger and Jeff more of your time so no one would notice how we felt about each other."

He grimaced. "I did say that."

"Then have you changed your mind? Have you decided that you don't want to keep your distance from me when we're around the others?"

"No. I still think we need to be careful in public. I'm talking about tonight. I don't want you to leave this room," he confessed in a low whisper. "The truth is, I'm not sure I can wait until Switzerland."

Before she knew what was happening, he reached for her and picked her up in his arms. She started to tremble because his eyes smoldered with raw desire.

"I want you, Whitney," he murmured against her mouth. "I want you so much it's agony."

She closed her eyes. *This was it.* He'd picked the time to make love to her and it was *now*.

He carried her to the twin bed and laid her down before sliding next to her. The next thing she knew he was kissing her like a man who was starving.

Keep your wits, Whitney. The recorder is picking up everything. When he starts to undress you, you'll have enough documentation to incriminate him. Then you can make an excuse why you have to go back to your room. Until you catch Mr. Bowen red-handed, you can't reveal what you're doing.

Whitney was so pliable and accommodating, it would be easy to forget they were anything but a man and woman enjoying each other for the sheer pleasure of it. In fact, Gerard was in danger of forgetting everything in the excitement of making love to her again.

Enticed by her warmth and softness, his lips ached to explore more beneath the collar of her blouse. That's when he came up against a small metal object which felt suspiciously like a mini microrecorder, the kind he wore when he was on assignment.

More curious than ever to know why she'd chosen him as her target, he decided now was as good a time as any to expose her and listen to her explanation. Slowly he slid his hands up her back and encircled her lovely neck.

His fingers made forays inside the rim of her collar. She must have sensed the gesture was more probing than wayward because she suddenly shifted in his arms, then pulled away from him. But she'd moved too late, giving him enough time to steal the device from its hiding place.

On his feet, he held it in the palm of his hand. She rolled off the bed to face him, her stare defiant.

"All right, Ms. Lawrence. I've been on to you for quite some time, and this little recorder is the additional proof I've needed before demanding an explanation. Do you want to start, or shall I?"

"Go ahead, Mr. Smith." Her icy smile was something to behold. "I've been waiting much longer than you for this day to come, and would love to watch you squirm your way out of it. Just remember, I've been wearing a recorder since we boarded the plane, and I have more than enough incriminating evidence to go to the authorities over your despicable conduct."

She was totally serious and he had no doubts she meant what she said.

"Who do you think I am?"

A caustic laugh escaped. "I know exactly who you are and what you've been doing for years and years, but you made a big mistake when you decided I would be your conquest for this particular trip."

One well-defined brow quirked. "*This* trip? Just how many trips do you think I've taken?"

"One too many."

He folded his arms and smiled at her. "It may interest you to know that this is my first tour with STI. Phone them right now if you like. They'll tell you I've never been on one of their tours before."

The silence started to stretch while she appeared to digest the veracity of his words. "Even if that were true," she came back hotly, "what you've been attempting to do to me is unconscionable. You're a criminal for taking advantage of a teenage girl while you're supposed to be chaperoning her throughout Europe!"

"But you're not a teenager, so that puts what we've both been doing to each other on another footing altogether. Wouldn't you say?"

The light began to dawn. He could see a flash of intelligence in her eyes. "Did that gendarme show you my passport?"

"He did. Technically I'm in charge of your welfare and he wanted to discuss you with me since you were one student who chose to stay in the hotel when the theft occurred. Luckily the police found the culprit, so you're no longer their chief suspect."

Again that very fascinating, clever brain of hers was

working overtime. "I don't believe there was a hotel theft. I think you made that up just to get a look."

He fought hard to suppress a smile. "You're free to think what you like. However, as it turns out, my office gave me all the background on you I needed. The newest junior attorney at Sharp and Rowe law firm in Salt Lake couldn't possibly be eighteen."

Her body stiffened in reaction. "Who are you?" she demanded in a low, barely controlled voice. "If you refuse to tell me, I can always have my colleague phone St. George to find out if a Hank Smith actually teaches there."

"You can do that, but you'll be told that I am employed there, so it would be a waste of energy to bother phoning. However, you're welcome to try."

She eyed the receiver, obviously debating whether to call his bluff or not. "Don't tell me. You're on this trip undercover for some reason."

"Let's just say that like you, I have an urgent reason to find out what is going on."

She had the grace to avert her eyes for a moment.

"Why don't we start over again. It's apparent you've been pretending to be a teenager to catch me in the act of compromising you. Why did you pick on me rather than Mr. Bowen?" At the mention of the other man's name, her head came up abruptly.

"You did want to be in his group. I distinctly remember your disappointment. What changed your mind? When he gave you the opportunity to switch groups, why did you decide to stay with me? I want an answer. You can either tell me here, in private, or we can go to the French authorities and you can be interrogated by them. It's your choice."

Her amazing violet eyes searched his for a long time. "Last year, my sister, Christine, came on this tour. A month after she got home, she told the family she was pregnant, but she refused to name the father. A couple of months ago she admitted that a man on her tour bus was the culprit. I figured it had to be her French teacher, or the tour guide or driver. So I signed up for the same tour to find out what I could."

Her explanation made perfect sense. "What caused you to think that I, rather than any of the other men, was the father of your nephew?"

To her credit, she didn't shy away from the question, or him. Eyeing him levelly she said, "Christine admitted he was a wonderful man who didn't force her. She also said he was very good-looking and she couldn't help falling in love. The only man on the tour with the kind of looks she was talking about had to be you."

Gerard supposed it was a compliment of sorts.

"I compared you to the other male teachers on the bus. For sheer masculine appeal, you won the contest hands down. Fran Ashton's interest in you convinced me you were the man I needed to nail. Such a monster deserves to be caught and prosecuted for what he did to my sister. He fathered her child and should be responsible for it!"

"I couldn't agree more."

She took what looked like a fortifying breath. "Christine always talked about Mr. Bowen, but your name never came up. I decided she'd purposely kept quiet about your existence so no one would ever suspect you were the father of her baby."

His brows drew together. "So you decided to come on to me and catch me in the act, so to speak."

The flush on her cheeks intensified, but she held her ground. "Yes. But something you said tonight, coupled with what happened to me today, made me realize I've been pursuing the wrong man. I know beyond the shadow of a doubt that you're not Christine's lover."

"Then that means you'll no longer be trying to seduce me?"

"That's right." She didn't bat an eye. Gerard felt his spirits plummet.

"Do you have an idea who the father is?"

"I know exactly who he is. By the time this tour is over, I'm going to have his head."

"Since you were with Mr. Bowen earlier today, I'm assuming he's your target."

"Whether he is or not, it's none of your business. From here on out, you do your thing and I'll do mine."

Lord. Everything had been pretense on her part.

Until now he'd felt mildly amused because he'd been so sure their attraction was a deeply mutual and satisfying thing. *Hell.*

"May I suggest we pool our resources and work together?"

She scowled at him. "Why would we do that? I can't very well seduce him with you about."

"That's true," he murmured testily. "But since I've come on this tour for the exclusive purpose of surveilling Mr. Bowen's activities, I thought we might be able to help each other."

"You've been spying on him?"

"That's right. Because of his flagrant interest in

you, it has made my job easier. Since you and I have managed to communicate rather well up to this point, I don't see what would prevent us from continuing as we have been." A dull red blush stained the rest of her face and neck, but she didn't look away. "After all," he said dryly, "we both want the same thing in the end."

"Did some parent hire you to make sure Mr. Bowen didn't seduce his daughter, too?" she fired back, ignoring his innuendos. Her question gave him the out he'd been looking for.

"Let's just say that there have been questions about him."

"Then that means my sister isn't the only teen to have been compromised by that sex-driven maniac." She sent him a withering glance. "If you were so busy tailing Mr. Bowen, how come you came on to me like an unscrupulous lothario?"

Her question stung. "Like you, Ms. Lawrence, I took one look at all the females on the tour and decided that if Bowen had seduction in mind, it would be with you rather than any of his girl students. Sure enough, before the film at the library was over, he tried to get me to trade you for one of his male students."

"He did?"

"That's right. Surely it's no surprise. You are very beautiful, you know."

She swallowed hard—the first sign that maybe she was more vulnerable to him than she'd been letting on.

"I thought that if I could get you to be interested in me, I could watch out for you and still force his hand."

"So you pretended to be interested in me in order to protect me."

"That's right. What I didn't count on was so much cooperation from you."

"Now you know why," she bit out.

He nodded, not liking her unspoken implication that there'd been no personal involvement on her part, that her breathtaking response to their lovemaking had been for business only. He couldn't accept that. He *wouldn't*.

"Since we understand each other completely, why don't we combine our efforts to bring him down. You tell me what you know about him, and I'll fill you in on what I've learned. Together we ought to be able to come up with a fairly foolproof plan."

She cocked her head. "What information do you have on him?"

"Not a great deal I'm afraid." He shifted his weight. "He's been taking these tours for the last six or seven years, and he always brings a mixture of teenage boys and girls along. His has a wife and child who never accompany him, and he only travels to France and Switzerland, which I find rather odd."

"I agree. You'd think that once in a while he would change the itinerary, but if it's seduction he has in mind every time, then he probably has certain haunts he can count on."

"Like the store he took you to this afternoon?" Gerard inserted. "Did you happen to notice if there was a hotel above the shop?"

She shook her head negatively. "I would assume they were apartments. Christine said he made love to her twice in his hotel room in Paris, both before and after she'd gone to pick up a package for him."

"What kind of package?"

"A toy for his daughter."

So the Moroccan souk was the contact point. "Whitney—why do you think he didn't go himself?"

"Christine said he was too sick to leave the room. Obviously he has a pattern of pretending to be ill to win his victim's sympathy. He certainly had her wrapped around his little finger. She was willing to do anything for him and said she'd go in his place. For a reward, he made love to her again. I can't help but wonder how many teenage girls this has happened to."

"Even more astounding is the fact that none of his victims tell on him."

"If they're anything like Christine, then they're too ashamed to admit what they've done. They know he's married with a child, so they are further intimidated. He told Christine he would contact her after the tour, but of course he never did."

"The man has no conscience," Gerard murmured, his thoughts leaping ahead. "What happened at the shop today? Did he buy anything?"

"No. He put a deposit down on a puppet he's going to pick up at the end of the tour."

"Did he pay in American or French money?"

She darted him another perplexed glance. "I have no idea. He handed the sales person a white envelope. Why do you want to know that?"

"I'm trying to figure out how the man operates to cover his tracks. If he's been doing this for six or seven years and hasn't been caught, then it means he's been very clever and devious. No doubt he's softening you up before he lures you to his hotel room and his bed.''

She nodded. "I'm positive that's what he has planned. He mentioned showing me some special places in Switzerland he's certain I'll appreciate.''

"Then we'll have to make sure he gets his way with you.''

"Thank heaven I'm down to seducing one man instead of two.''

Gerard grimaced, not liking the sound of that at all. *She couldn't have forgotten what it felt like when they got into each other's arms.*

"For the rest of the trip I'll give him enough rope to almost hang himself. When we reach Paris, I'll set the trap and get everything on tape before I tell him who I am, that the game is up.''

"I'll be right there to help you tighten the noose,'' Gerard assured her. *I'll be right there to do a lot more than that, Ms. Lawrence.*

"First off, I think that after the bus leaves Versailles for Dijon tomorrow, I'll arrange things so that you end up sitting next to him. That way he'll feel free to make further plans with you. From here on out, we want to stay a couple of steps ahead of him in case he tries to do something unexpected.''

"Don't worry. Whatever that man pulls, I'll be ready for him. By the way, what's your real name?''

He followed her to the door, but it was all he could do not to pull her back into his arms. "Eric-Gerard,'' he whispered, "but forget you heard it or you'll ruin my cover. *Dors bien.*''

Sleep well.

His husky voice permeated to her very insides as

she crept to her room on shaky legs and fell back against the closed door.

She'd had to pretend so many things in front of him. Now that she was alone, her body and emotions were reacting to the shocking revelation that Hank Smith's real name was Eric-Gerard. It was humiliating to realize how impulsive she'd been in her decision to throw herself at him.

Because of the way he operated, the speed with which he'd learned about her background, she assumed he had to be some kind of undercover officer masquerading as a French teacher. Obviously Whitney wasn't the only person who suspected Mr. Bowen was taking advantage of the female students, and wanted him caught. She should be relieved there was someone else working on her side.

But since that first night at the library, she'd been flirting shamelessly with him, never realizing he knew who she really was. He'd lead her on the entire time. *Had he run a background check on her before they ever left Salt Lake?*

It humiliated her to realize she was the only one who had become emotionally involved. A man could make love to a woman without it meaning much more than a pleasurable interlude which was soon forgotten. While Eric-Gerard alias Hank Smith had been doing what he perceived needed doing to keep an eye on Mr. Bowen—mainly responding to Whitney's physical overtures—Whitney had made the fatal mistake of falling in love with him.

How else could she explain these feelings? He'd knocked the foundation out from under her, even when she'd believed the worst about him.

White-hot heat enveloped her body when she thought about how she'd responded to his lovemaking. One touch of his hand, one kiss had turned her into a wanton, uninhibited woman who'd clung to him, practically begging him to continue that mindless ecstasy and never stop.

Somehow she was going to have to feign indifference when they were alone, yet keep the same student-teacher relationship with him when they were in public.

She hurriedly got ready for bed, but sleep was impossible because she knew Hank was on the other side of the hotel room wall separating them. Her body still writhed with unassuaged longings. If he hadn't discovered that minirecorder when he did...

Whitney sat up in bed abruptly, her heart racing out of rhythm. The fantasies had to stop. That's all they were. Creations of her imagination which had no basis in reality.

Hank Smith—that was the name she'd better stick to—had come on this tour because it was his job. If Mr. Bowen had picked on one of the other female students to seduce, Hank would have intervened on that poor teen's behalf instead of Whitney's.

In that particular instance, he would have treated Whitney like he treated Jeff and Roger. Whitney would never have known the kind of incredible intimacy they'd shared over the last few days. What hurt most was to realize his lovemaking had been part of a day's work, nothing more.

She needed to get that into her head. Above all, she

couldn't let on that what had transpired between them had affected her in any way whatsoever.

The best thing for her to do was concentrate on Mr. Bowen and set him up for the kill. Discovering the father of Christine's baby was the sole reason she'd come on this tour in the first place. Now that she knew his identity, she could lay the trap she'd been planning and use Hank, rather than the local police, for backup.

Tomorrow, while they drove to Dijon, she would make herself available to Mr. Bowen and follow his lead, wherever it took her. The thought of him touching her, let alone kissing her, made her cringe in revulsion, but at some point she was going to have to allow him those liberties or her plan would fail.

On a groan she turned over on her stomach, determined to empty her mind of everything and get some sleep before her alarm went off.

But as she would come to find out in the nights ahead, she had little control over her thoughts. Right now all that consumed her was the man next door.

Who was he really? He'd referred to an office. Did he work in Salt Lake? Was it true about his being free? Was he divorced, or a widower? Or did he have a wife? A man as attractive as he was would have been claimed by a beautiful, desirable woman a long time ago.

If he was married, how did she stand to let her husband go off on undercover assignments, never knowing what he did when he was away from her, never knowing if and when he became physically involved with another woman as part of his latest assignment.

Whitney could never abide such an arrangement. She knew herself far too well. If a man like Hank

Smith were her husband, she wouldn't be able to share him. Not for any reason or under any circumstances.

All worked up again, she buried her face in the pillow. Right now she'd sell her soul to know if he was thinking thoughts about her, and more particularly, if those thoughts made it difficult for him to sleep…

CHAPTER NINE

"HANK SMITH, as I live and breathe! Imagine bumping into you here of all places."

Keeping one eye trained on Whitney who was standing by the railing with Jeff and Roger taking pictures, Gerard had been lounging with the other teachers in their group aboard the steamer that cruised Lake Geneva when he heard Yuri's distinctive voice call out to him in impeccable French.

Removing his sunglasses, Gerard levered himself from the deck chair and gave his good friend a bear hug. Yuri reciprocated in kind. They grinned at each other, sending nonverbal messages. It had been too long since they'd last seen each other.

Rather than choose the hotel restaurant in Geneva where Donald Bowen could excuse himself and walk out on everyone when he chose, Gerard and Yuri had decided ahead of time that the boat would be the best place for a reunion and introductions.

No one could go anywhere until it made its first scheduled stop around the lake at Lausanne, a city the students were going to explore. But that wouldn't be for another half hour at least. Enough time for Yuri to make a judgment about Bowen's ethnic background.

"Eh bien, mes amis," Gerard provided the introductions in French. "This is Dr. Antoine LeCler, an old ski buddy of mine from way back when I lived in Europe. He's originally from Charleroi, and is now a

144

professor of languages in Geneva. Hey, Don? You remember my telling you about my friend?''

Bowen, taken completely by surprise, hesitated before saying, ''But of course.''

Gerard couldn't have been happier with the situation.

''Antoine? Don here studied in Charleroi for a time. You both have the same accent.''

Everyone agreed and soon Yuri and Bowen were plied with the kinds of questions only Francophiles who lived and breathed everything French would ask.

Yuri played his role like a pro, drawing everyone into the conversation, forcing Bowen to respond when it was obvious to Gerard that the other man didn't want this kind of attention.

Each teacher exchanged French anecdotes, telling funny personal experiences. Even Fran Ashton shed her hostility toward Gerard long enough to enter in.

Yuri, who could do amazing language imitations, had a way about him that invited secret confessions and laughter. The only person who didn't appear caught up in their lively discussion was Bowen. This prompted Yuri to go for the jugular, making it impossible for Bowen to avoid his share of the unwanted limelight.

Donning his sunglasses once more, Gerard searched the crowds of students for Whitney who had moved out of his line of vision. Since that illuminating scene in his hotel room night before last, she'd left him alone while she mingled more and more with Bowen's students to allow their target easier access to her. As a result, she rarely gave Gerard the time of day.

Not once during an unguarded moment had he

caught her looking at him with that hint of longing. When their eyes did meet, she regarded him head-on, the way she did everyone else, giving away nothing of her thoughts.

By her seeming disinterest, the desire that had engulfed them from the beginning might never have been. But Gerard couldn't fathom that all those feelings and emotions had been pretense on her part. Before he went to bed tonight, he was going to catch her unaware and elicit the response he'd been waiting for. *Living for.*

"Eh bien, mon ami." Yuri spoke loud enough to Gerard so everyone could hear. "What are the chances of you visiting my summer language camp at Clarens? That's where I'm headed this morning."

"Much as I would like that, I can't leave my students."

"I'll watch them." Bowen jumped in on cue ahead of the others. He'd seen the perfect opportunity to get Whitney to himself and didn't waste a moment. Now that he didn't feel Gerard was trying to thwart him, Bowen was showing a more magnanimous spirit.

"You're sure?"

The other man shrugged. "Three more students is nothing. It isn't every day you meet up with an old friend."

"Thanks, Don. I owe you."

"Forget it. It's my pleasure. Take the whole day off. We'll see you back at the hotel tonight for the polka fest."

Gerard smiled. *"Fantastique.* Excuse me a moment while I go find my students and tell them of the change in plans." He motioned to Yuri. "Come with me,

Antoine. I'll introduce you. They'll be impressed to meet an old ski bum who turned out to be a scholar of such high repute.''

"Be careful, *mon ami*. Don't forget I know stories about you that could ruin your reputation.''

Yuri's remark left everyone chuckling as Gerard motioned to his good friend to follow him up the stairs to the next deck.

As soon as they were out of sight of the others Yuri whispered, "He's from one of the old Eastern Block countries, like Romania. No question about it.''

"Then everything fits," Gerard murmured. "There's a faction from that area of the continent working for an emerging Arab nation. Undoubtedly some military secrets stolen from the Americans are being funneled through that shop in Paris. They're using a Moroccan cover. Bowen has been their go-between for six years, and uses one of his students every time to make the final contact.''

"If you'd stayed with Interpol, Monsieur Bowen's cover would have been blown five years sooner. But luckily for me and Roman, you gave all that up and came back to Utah to live.''

"Amen to that, Yuri. I have no interest in doing anything more than staying home and continuing the undercover work I like best.''

Yuri darted him a shrewd glance. "Haven't you left something out?''

"What do you mean?''

"Come on. "Fess up. Roman's been telling me about a very fetching eighteen-year-old high school student named Whitney Lawrence you've gotten involved with. Shame on you, *Comradsky*.''

Gerard groaned. "That information was classified."

"So was Roman's bogus marriage to Brittany when he was working undercover as her husband to catch the man stalking her. But that didn't stop you from leaving out one very important detail when you let that bomb drop on me that he was getting married…"

"I've already repented of that particular sin. Besides they're very happily married *now*."

"They are, *thank God*. But I haven't quite forgiven you yet for jumping the gun and telling me they were legally married when they *weren't!* So tell me about this forbidden infant goddess who has brought you to your knees. I never thought I'd see the day." He rubbed his hands, relishing the moment. "Roman is expecting a detailed report."

"She's not an infant, *Comrade*. She's a twenty-six-year-old attorney."

"But you didn't know that at the beginning, you old reprobate."

"You don't know the half of it," he half growled. "There she is now, by the railing. The one in the print skirt and blouse with the—"

"Blond hair and long legs that go on forever?" Yuri interrupted. "I see her." He whistled. "No wonder you found yourself in so much trouble." Yuri's voice trailed as Gerard turned swiftly away and started across the promenade deck to the place where she was standing with the guys.

"Whitney? Jeff? Roger?"

All three turned around. "Hi, Hank. What's up?" Roger asked.

Gerard noticed with increasing frustration that Whitney remained silent, her regard impersonal.

"I'd like you three to meet a very old, close friend of mine, Dr. Antoine LeCler. We did a lot of skiing together in Europe years ago."

Everyone said hello and shook hands.

"Antoine has invited me to spend some time with him today, so Mr. Bowen has offered to show you guys around Lausanne with his students if that's okay."

"Sure." Jeff spoke up, nudging Roger because both boys were excited about the idea of being around Whitney without Gerard breathing down their necks.

"Is that all right with you, Whitney?" he prodded because she still hadn't said anything. Instead, those violet eyes were studying Yuri, probably trying to figure out where he fit into the scheme of things. Suddenly she switched her enigmatic gaze to Gerard.

"Of course."

Her mouth was so enticing, Gerard had a hard time keeping his eyes level with hers. To his chagrin, she didn't appear to have any problem facing him. *Hell.*

"Then I'll see you back at the hotel in Geneva for dinner."

"Enjoy yourself, Hank. We'll watch out for Whitney," Jeff assured him. "Nice to have met you, Dr. LeCler."

Yuri shook everyone's hand. "The pleasure was all mine. Thanks for letting me steal my old buddy away for the day. We have a lot of catching up to do."

"Be good and don't spend too much money," Gerard flung them a final warning. As he turned away, he thought he saw Whitney shiver. Since the heat was fairly intense on this beautiful summer day, he suspected she was dreading the thought of spending any time with Bowen, no matter how anxious she was to expose him.

Gratified that she'd shed a little of that sangfroid, enough to show some adverse reaction to his imminent departure because she thought she was going to be on her own with Bowen, Gerard descended to the lower deck with Yuri in a better frame of mind than he'd experienced in several days.

"So, *Comradsky*—it looks like we're coming in to dock. Wish we could spend some real time together."

Gerard clapped him on the shoulder. "In four days this case will be wound up. If I can, I'll stop in New York on my way home."

"I'm counting on it. Something tells me that when you get back to Salt Lake with Ms. Lawrence, I won't be able to pry you away for a weekend, let alone a holiday."

His jaw hardened. "I'm not sure she's interested."

"Then you must be blind."

"How so?"

Yuri stared at him through veiled eyes. "The tension between you two could light up a city. You have the same kind of chemistry I felt around Roman and Brittany when they were both pretending that they weren't emotionally involved with each other. You can try to hide it all you want, but the vibes are there."

"I wish I could believe you."

"After you've caught Bowen, you'll be able to see more clearly."

"That day can't come soon enough." He turned to Yuri. "Thanks for being there for me."

Yuri flashed him a white smile, reminding Gerard

of Roman. "What are friends for? Shall we go? Everyone's debarking."

Gerard nodded and the two men moved toward the gangplank. "What's your plan?"

"I phoned ahead to the hotel over there. They have a rental car waiting for me to drive back to Geneva. My flight home leaves in an hour and a half. I guess you have your work cut out following Bowen around."

"That's right. No telling what he has in mind now that he thinks he's got Whitney to himself for the whole day," Gerard ground out, his gaze focused on the back of the woman who had brought him alive in a way he'd never experienced before.

He and Yuri stepped off the boat behind everyone else and waited until the tour group had rounded a corner before Gerard took leave of his good friend and started after them.

For the next six hours he followed every move Bowen made with the students through shops, restaurants, churches and parks, but he didn't see him pull anything out of the ordinary to get Whitney alone.

Gerard figured that with the other teachers and students around, Bowen's hands were pretty much tied for the day. Of course that wouldn't prevent him from making private plans with Whitney, plans Gerard would hear about later when he took Whitney aside.

By five o'clock, the group boarded the train headed back to Geneva. Gerard took a taxi from the station to the hotel so he could reach his room ahead of Whitney. With hers straight across the hall from his, he could leave his door slightly ajar and listen to any conversation that might ensue.

He waited five minutes before he heard Jeff's and Roger's familiar voices in the hall, Whitney's among them. It didn't appear Bowen was with them since his room was one floor up.

As soon as all was quiet, Gerard gave Whitney a few more minutes, then he slipped across the hall and tapped on her door.

"Who is it?"

Pleased that she had learned not to open her door to anyone before calling out, he said, "It's Hank. I need to talk to you."

Just the sound of his low, male voice made Whitney quiver with excitement. Aside from the fact that she needed to talk to him about Mr. Bowen, she craved his company. Being apart from him for a whole day had shown her unequivocally how much he'd come to mean to her, how much she wanted and needed him in her life. It was frightening how one man had transformed her world forever.

But she was quite sure he didn't feel the same way about her. He had a job to do, and when it was done, she feared she would never see him again.

Right now she needed time to compose herself before she let him in. The way she was feeling, she wanted to fling herself into his arms and never let go.

Instead, she pressed herself against the door. "Couldn't we talk on the phone just as easily? I—I need to shower."

"Let me in, Whitney."

She blinked. He sounded so intense, she wouldn't put it past him to enter her room anyway.

With shaky hands she undid the lock. He swept inside and shoved the door closed with his foot, bringing the faint scent of the soap he used with him.

She felt his penetrating gaze envelope her in one all-encompassing glance, sending a wave of heat over her body. While she looked her worst in the limp blouse and skirt she'd been wearing all day, he sported a navy polo shirt and khakis, and had never appeared more attractive. His appeal hit her like a physical force.

"Tell me what went on with Bowen today. I tailed you everywhere, so I know he didn't try to separate you from the others."

Her eyes widened. "You followed us?"

"That's right."

"But your friend—"

"My friend was helping me with this case. By now he's back in New York with his family."

Whitney studied his rugged features. "He's not a professor of languages."

"No, though he's a master of half a dozen. What plans does Bowen have for you?"

Whitney lowered her eyes. It was just as she thought. All he cared about was the case.

"Several things actually. Since tomorrow is a free morning, he wanted to take me to a resort on the French side of the lake for breakfast. He said something about renting a car."

"Did you say you would go?"

She lifted her eyes to his once more, noting how much greener they'd suddenly become.

"No. I pretended that I had already made plans to do shopping with friends. That's when he told me that he had developed indigestion after eating cheese fondue for lunch and was planning to skip dinner and the polka fest they're staging here tonight.''

"Which is a lie. He's moving in on you now and doesn't want to wait until Paris.''

Whitney groaned at the prospect of having to tolerate the other man's touch even for an instant. "I don't want to wait until Paris, either. I'd just a soon get this over with tonight.''

"For reasons I can't go into now, it's imperative you put him off until the end of the trip.''

Her head reared back. "Why?''

His expression hardened. "Because there's more at stake here than catching this man in the middle of committing an immoral act with an innocent teenager.''

Starting to put two and two together she asked, "Are you an FBI agent or something?''

"No, Ms. Lawrence. I'm a private detective working with Interpol, and that's as much as I'm free to tell you.''

Dear God. She really didn't mean anything to him. She had just happened to get in the middle of a sting operation, and he'd decided to make use of her.

The knowledge hurt. It hurt more than anything had ever hurt her in her whole life.

"I presume Mr. Bowen is a wanted man and considered dangerous,'' she said in a brittle voice. She couldn't help it.

He straightened to his full height. "As long as you do exactly as I say until we reach Paris, there is absolutely no fear for your safety.''

I'm not worried about my safety. You stole my heart and have changed my life forever.

"Do I have a choice?"

"Of course, but you'd be doing your country a great service if you were willing to play along."

My country?

"What I want you to do," he drawled, appearing to read her mind, "is string him along until we reach Paris and he asks you to pick up that toy for his daughter. Since you turned him down for tomorrow, no doubt he's intending to lure you to his room tonight on some pretext or other."

Whitney folded her arms tightly against her waist. "The same thought crossed my mind."

"When he calls, follow his lead and go to his room so he'll believe you're interested in getting more intimate with him. I'll give you a few minutes, then create a diversion that will interrupt anything he has in mind."

"Don't wait too long!" she blurted before she realized how much she had admitted by that telling outburst.

When she'd been seducing Hank, the last thing she had worried about was the time. She'd come across as a wanton lover in his arms and had shown no reticence whatsoever. And Hank *knew* it.

As if to make matters worse, the phone rang just then, jarring her nerves so badly she actually jumped. The realization that Mr. Bowen was in pursuit of her made her ill, especially now that Hank had shed new light on the situation.

The man who'd changed her world for all time darted her a surprisingly fierce glance before motioning for her to pick up the receiver.

With trepidation she reached for it and said hello.

"Whitney? It's Donald Bowen."

"I was just about to call you and see how you were feeling."

"How sweet of you. Unfortunately, I'n not doing very well."

"Oh, dear. Then you'll miss the show tonight."

"I'm afraid so. Say, I was wondering if after dinner you would mind bringing me some tea. They don't have room service here and I think I need something to settle my stomach."

"I'd love to bring you tea, and anything else you might like. Shall I pick up an antacid at the pharmacy?"

"Oh, no. That won't be necessary. Tea ought to do the trick. But I hate taking you away from the polka fest."

"Oh, Mr. Bowen. After all the nice things you've done for me, do you think I care about that? It will be a pleasure to help you. I ought to be at your room within the hour. Where is it?"

"Number sixteen on the third floor. You're a treasure, Whitney. I'm looking forward to seeing you,"

"Me, too. À tout à l'heure."

She put down the receiver. "Did I do that right?"

One dark blond brow arched sardonically. "So right the man won't waste any time making his move once you're alone with him."

A shudder passed through her body. "I think I'm going to skip dinner."

She felt his probing gaze wander over her features. "I tell you what. You relax and do whatever you feel like. I'll go downstairs and tell the guys you have a headache. After I've eaten dinner, I'll bring the tea to your room and you can proceed from there.''

"Fine. Now if you'll excuse me, I need to shower."

He didn't move. "Whitney? You don't need to worry. I'll be here to protect you every step of the way."

"I'm not worried," she lied. "I just want to get out of these clothes."

She thought she saw a bleak look enter his eyes before he made a swift exit from the room and shut the door quietly behind him.

She raced to the door to lock it, then threw herself across the twin bed and sobbed into the pillow. This trip had turned into a nightmare.

Forty minutes later, after Gerard had made a call to his contact at Interpol and had joined the boys for dinner, he took the tray of tea and rolls to Whitney's room.

He was close to solving this case, but part of him wished he could go back to a few days ago when Whitney had no idea what was going on and had melted in his arms whenever they found an opportunity to get close.

She couldn't have been playacting all the time. He'd stake his life and reputation on the fact that she had wanted him as much as he'd wanted her.

But the wooden-faced woman who opened the door just now gave nothing of those feelings away. She'd obviously freshened up and changed into black pants and a frothy white blouse her figure did wonders for. The fragrance from the shampoo she used filled the hallway. That purely professional manner of hers tore at his emotions, leaving him feeling at loose ends and dangerously restless.

Without a word to him, she took the tray and left for Bowen's room. Gerard went to his own room and maintained contact through his cellular phone with the agents who'd come to the hotel on the pretext of investigating another theft. He instructed them to give her five minutes from the time she went inside before they knocked on Bowen's door and asked her to go back to her room for her passport.

Five minutes wasn't enough time for her to get into too much trouble, but he wasn't about to take any chances where she was concerned. Bowen had no conscience and would be ruthless now that he believed he was this close to getting Whitney under his complete control.

It felt more like five hours before she came back to the room. When she saw him, she let out an audible gasp, as if he were the last person she expected to see. *Or wanted to see. Lord.*

"How did it go? Did he try to get physical with you?" Gerard hoped his voice didn't betray his emotions, which were churning at the idea of Bowen or any other man touching her.

She refused to look at him.

"He got up from the bed and took the tray from me. Then he kissed my forehead and told me I was angel."

"That was all?" Gerard prodded because she was no longer forthcoming. His eyes followed the movement of her hands which were rubbing her hips absently, revealing a high degree of agitation.

"No."

He took a step closer to her. "What else did he do to you?"

"He didn't try to make love to me, if that's what you mean. It was what he said."

Gerard sucked in his breath. "Go on."

"He admitted that his marriage had been over for a long time, and that he'd been fighting his feelings for me because I was so young. But he said it was no use. He'd fallen in love with me and wanted to make love to me. He wanted to know if I felt the same way."

Gerard's hands tightened into fists. "And you said?"

"I told him that I would never have come to his room with the tea if I didn't feel a strong attraction, too."

"You think he believed you?"

She whirled around, her cheeks flushed. "I made sure he did."

Certain pictures ran through his mind, filling him with rage. That swine had kissed her mouth and held her in his arms. Adrenaline surged through his taut body.

"What plans did he make with you before you were interrupted?"

"The gendarme pounded on the door too soon for us to talk about anything."

That was the best news Gerard had heard all night.

"Now that the proverbial die has been cast, you realize that in a few minutes your phone will ring and he'll ask you to come back to his room to take up where you left off."

She nodded jerkily. "Either that, or he'll decide to come to my room, confident that I'll let him in."

Gerard heard more than a trace of fear in her tone just now.

"Well, he won't find you here. Since you're a student on this tour and it's your legitimate right to be with the group, we're going to join everyone downstairs for the festivities and there's nothing he can say or do about it. His hands are firmly tied, at least for tonight." *Thank heaven.* "Shall we go?"

Without waiting for an answer, he cupped her elbow and ushered her from the room, relishing her warmth. In her near-panic state, she didn't seem to mind the contact.

Or else she's so upset she hasn't noticed, an inner voice tortured him as they made their way down the hall and subsequent two flights of stairs to the dining hall.

The group of dancers in native Swiss costume backed by musicians with accordians were in the middle of a lively routine when he and Whitney worked their way to the table where Jeff and Roger were seated.

The guys were delighted to have her back and made a place for her between them, leaving Gerard to take a seat on the opposite side of the table next to Mr. Hart and his group.

To make certain any plans Bowen had for Whitney were totally thwarted once the performance was over, Gerard invited the boys and Whitney to take a walk along the water's edge and enjoy the balmy night air.

For Jeff and Roger the evening turned out to be a total success, replete with a stop at the world-famous House of Chocolate where they all splurged on truffles and bought gifts to take home to their families.

As for Whitney, he knew she was thankful to be away from the hotel where Bowen couldn't get to her. But whether she found pleasure in being with Gerard for a few hours, he had no way of knowing, not when she involved herself in the boys' conversations for the duration of their outing.

However, when they all said good night in the hall, she couldn't quite hide her anxiety at being alone again. He watched the animation vanish from her face just before she shut the door to her room.

As soon as everyone disappeared, Gerard stepped across the hall and called her name.

She opened the door a crack. "What is it?"

"A word of warning. Don't answer your phone tonight."

"I—I won't."

He'd told her too much about Bowen. Now she was feeling more vulnerable than ever and it was all his fault. *Damn.*

"This is almost over, Whitney. We just have to get you through tomorrow night in Strasbourg, then we'll be back in Paris where he'll ask you to pick up the toy for him. When that transaction has taken place, Bowen will be placed in custody and you'll never have to see him again."

"Tomorrow night is what's worrying me." Her voice betrayed a tremor.

"There's no reason to be nervous. I've arranged to take you and the boys on a little side trip over the border into Germany. If Bowen raises objections to your going, you can tell him the plans were made days ago and can't be altered, but remind him you'll spend all your time with him when you get to Paris."

She bit her lower lip. "That sounds like a good plan."

He could read between the lines. "You're frightened about tonight, aren't you?"

Her expression closed up. "If he knocks on my door, I'll ignore him."

"That's right," he ground out, coming to a lightning decision. "Because you won't be in here."

Her eyes widened. "What do you mean?"

"From now on you're going to sleep in my room until this case is closed. Grab what you need for tonight."

"But—"

"Don't question my judgment, Whitney. I know things you don't and prefer to protect you at close range."

"You think I need protecting?"

"I'm not sure. We're dealing with an unknown here. Let's just say I'll be able to do my job better if I know you're safe with me. I would have suggested this arrangement sooner, but didn't want to upset you unduly. Where's your key?"

She acted shell-shocked. "On the dresser."

Face it, Roche. The lady's not interested in being alone with you, but that's too damn bad because you're spending the rest of your nights with her anyway.

When this case is over, you can take a nice, long vacation at Yuri's until you get Ms. Lawrence completely out of your system.

But a few minutes later as he followed her out of the room and locked it, he was seized by the haunting fear that she had a permanent hold on his heart and there wasn't anything he could do about it.

"You can sleep in my bed," he muttered as they entered his room seconds later.

She whirled around. "Where will you sleep?"

"I have a bedroll. Go ahead and make yourself comfortable. I've got some business to take care of so I'm going downstairs for a while. Lock the door behind me. I have a key, and will let myself in later. See you in the morning. *Dors bien.*"

CHAPTER TEN

WHITNEY couldn't believe this was happening to her. She was actually going to spend the night with Hank.

Right now her emotions had risen to such a feverish pitch, she was running on nerves and little else.

This was a mistake. She knew it was, but part of her exulted in the fact that she was going to be with him, no matter the reason. In a few days it would all be over. Hank would receive another assignment, wherever that was, and Whitney would get back to the law firm. In no time she would be immersed in the case she'd been working on before she left.

As for telling Christine that the father of her baby was not only an unscrupulous liar, but a man wanted by Interpol for crimes against his country, Whitney had already made the decision to say nothing to her sister or family about this trip.

Christine had been trying to put the whole affair behind her. She had the right to keep a few illusions and raise her son without knowing the sordid details of Donald Bowen's double life.

Greg was an adorable, innocent little boy with a body and spirit all his own. Whitney would never burden him or his mother with ugly details that could serve no purpose and only bring pain. This whole trip was best forgotten.

Except that you'll never forget it, Whitney. You'll never forget him...

Taking advantage of the time alone, she reached for her cosmetic bag and cotton flannel robe, then rushed into the adjoining cubicle to get ready for bed. She wasn't sure that sometime during the night she would be able to stop herself from climbing into his bed and begging him to make love to her for the time they had left.

Until she'd met Hank, Whitney would never have imagined such a situation happening to her where she would do anything for a man's love, knowing full well he didn't return her feelings.

It was a good thing this trip was almost over, her mind repeated like a litany. But her heart kept pounding out a different message as she lay there listening for his footsteps.

To her surprise, the next thing she knew it was morning and she awakened to an empty room. Hank had made her feel so safe, she'd fallen into oblivion without realizing it. If he'd slept on the floor by the bed, she saw no sleeping bag. For that matter, his luggage was gone. He'd probably taken it down to the bus.

The only evidence that he'd been in the room was the message he'd left for her on the dresser.

Whitney—
Bowen paid you a little call last night. When he couldn't gain entrance, he slipped a note under your door. He has plans for you tonight, but as we discussed earlier, you're not going to be around. Remain in my room until I come for you.

Hank.

Did that mean he'd stayed up most of the night keeping guard? When did he sleep? *Had he watched her?*

Alternate shivers of consternation and excitement raced through her body.

Needing to give vent to emotions the very thought of him aroused, she got out of bed and dressed quickly in a clean pair of pants and blouse so she'd be ready for him.

She longed to wear clothes befitting her age and taste. It would be wonderful to apply makeup and arrange her hair in its normal style. In truth, she wanted Hank to see her as the twenty-six-year-old woman she was. But until the tour was over she had to continue her eighteen-year-old disguise.

Her heart ached to realize that she might never see him again after this. He would never know her as her family and friends did.

"Whitney?" he called out ten minutes later, breaking into her torturous thoughts. She heard the key in the lock before he opened the door.

She donned her sunglasses, afraid to meet his searching gaze. "I—I'm ready," she stammered. At this point she was behaving as outrageously as any lovesick teen on the trip.

Grabbing her cases, she slipped out of the room, past his hard-muscled body. He relieved her of them as they walked side by side down the hall to the stairs.

"I'll put these on the bus after you've gone. Sorry you're going to miss breakfast. A bunch of kids are waiting for you in the foyer to go shopping. Don't come back until lunch. We'll be boarding the bus for Strasbourg directly after we eat. I'll be with the guys.

We'll follow you through town at a discreet distance. Have a good day.''

"You, too," she muttered, and hurried down the steps alone to the hotel lobby where a large group of students were congregated with a couple of teachers, Donald Bowen included. To her relief, she was surrounded by so many of the tour group, he couldn't take her aside without drawing unwanted attention.

Throughout their morning-long souvenir hunt and lunch on the hotel terrace, she made sure he never got close enough to make any remarks for her ears alone.

When it came time to board the bus, Hank was there ahead of schedule, holding three seats for her and the boys. She sat with Roger and pretended interest in his postcards until Donald Bowen passed them in the aisle.

They didn't reach Strasbourg until seven that evening. After their tour group settled in the hotel, Hank arranged for a minivan to take them and several other students over the border into Germany for a Wiener schnitzel dinner followed by mouth-watering apple strudel and a German slap-dancing show for the tourists.

Hank was as fluent in German as French and kept up a running monologue of hilarious language anecdotes until everyone was convulsed in laughter. Despite her fears of what lay ahead, Whitney couldn't remember when she'd been so entertained.

It was all because of their fascinating, intelligent, sophisticated host and chaperone whose charisma charmed young and old alike. There weren't enough adjectives to describe him. She was so in love with him it terrified her.

They didn't arrive back at their hotel until well after midnight. Whitney couldn't wait to be alone with him, but that didn't happen until everyone had said goodnight. When the hall was clear, he motioned for her to come next door to his room with her things.

In the dimly lit interior his attractive face appeared darker. The laughter and funning had long since gone to be replaced by a sober expression. The man facing her looked big and powerful. *Dangerous.*

"All right," he murmured in gravelly tones, straddling the only chair while she sat down on the end of the bed. His eyes narrowed on her features.

"Here's the plan. Once we arrive in Paris tomorrow, go straight to your room and stay there. You'll be watched every minute, and you'll be wearing a listening device to pick up all conversation with Bowen. I'll leave it out for you to put on in the morning.

"This is one time when I can't tell you what to do. You'll have to play it by ear. If he tries to come on too strong or attempts to overpower you, I'll be right next door ready to run interference."

She nodded jerkily.

"Remember this... As much as he wants to make love to you, he *must* carry out his transaction and will stop at nothing to accomplish his objective. Because of your desirability, you've been chosen as his tool this trip.

"Try to act natural and follow his instructions. A vulnerable eighteen-year-old in love with him would never ask questions or show undue interest in his private business. He'll probably send you to the shop by taxi.

"Rest assured that undercover police will be all

over the hotel and all over the shop. The second you pay for the package and start to leave with it, the shop owner and Bowen will be arrested. Neither you or innocent victims like your sister will ever have to deal with him again.''

''Thank heaven.''

''Amen. Now I suggest we both get some sleep. We're going to need it.''

With a sense of déjà vu, she got ready for bed wearing the same flannel robe as the night before. She disappeared into the bathroom after he did. While she was otherwise occupied, he rolled out his sleeping bag near the door. Once she crossed the room and had slid under the covers, he turned out the lights.

She'd only been given a glimpse of his magnificent physique clothed in a T-shirt and sweats. It was enough to keep her awake for the rest of the night.

The man on the floor didn't seem to have the same problem. Within minutes she could heard the slow, even tenor of his breathing. He sounded like someone in the deepest throes of much-needed sleep.

Because he'd been so busy playing chaperone, keeping her safe and tailing Donald Bowen at the same time, she doubted he'd had any rest to speak of throughout the entire trip.

The great personal sacrifices he made on a routine basis as a PI, and more particularly on this tour, brought out her most compassionate instincts as nothing else could do.

For the rest of the night she lay on her left side so she could keep a close vigil over him. Throughout the dark hours she allowed her wildest fantasies free rein until she heard his alarm and watched his long legs stir beneath the protection of his bag.

She loved him with all her heart. Now that he'd been able to rest without interruption, she felt content and turned on her other side to give him his privacy. The next thing she knew, she felt a strong hand on her shoulder urging her to wake up.

On a groan, she rolled over and surprised those little green lights in his beautiful gray eyes, the same burst of illumination she'd seen in that sensuous gaze the first time she'd caught him staring at her.

She couldn't catch her breath. *"Hank?"* she finally whispered. "W-what time is it?"

Just as quickly, his eyes grew shuttered. He raked a hand through his dark blond hair and straightened to his full height.

"Almost seven. Everyone will be boarding the bus in a few minutes. You're going to have to hustle if you want any breakfast. I'll meet you downstairs. No doubt Bowen has arranged for you to sit by him on the drive to Paris. Do it willingly."

He started to leave, then paused midstride. "Whitney?" There was an unusual cadence in his tone.

"Yes?"

"Be careful."

"I was going to say the same thing to you," she responded in an aching voice.

After he left the room she died a little inside because he hadn't said the words she craved to hear.

And what words would those be, Whitney?

This is just a day's work to him. As you've found out, he's an honorable man. Not once did he try to take advantage of you or make a move toward you.

Not once did he suggest there could be a future. Face it. You mean nothing to him personally. Get over him or it will destroy you.

"Donald? Are you sure you're not too sick for a visitor? On the bus I was so worried about you."

"You don't need to be, Whitney. I'm fine. Come over here on the bed and let me have a good look at you."

Perspiration beaded Gerard's forehead as he listened to their conversation from the room next door to Bowen's.

"Is this close enough?"

"No."

No more words were forthcoming. Only breathing noises, little moans and groans, the rustle of sheets, the sounds of two people kissing each other in passion.

Gerard felt bile rise in his throat. Pictures filled his mind until all he could see was blackness.

"Are you frightened?"

"No. Not exactly. Yes."

Bowen's low laughter filled Gerard with such rage, he knew he wasn't going to let Whitney sacrifice herself this way much longer. To hell with the assignment. This was one time he didn't care if he blew his cover.

"How adorable you are. How incredibly sweet and beautiful."

"You're beautiful to me, too, Donald."

Whitney's acting was so superb, Gerard couldn't believe she wasn't an agent. Now was the time to put his second plan into action. Without hesitation he rang Bowen's room on the hotel phone.

Seconds later Gerard could hear Bowen's phone ringing.

"Don't make a sound, Whitney."

Gerard could visualize Bowen reaching for the phone.

"Oui?" came the terse greeting.

"Don? It's Gerard. We've all been worried about you. How's your stomach?"

"Better now that I'm lying down."

He gripped the receiver tighter. "I've asked the kitchen to prepare you some warm milk and tapioca pudding. It works for me when my ulcer acts up."

"You shouldn't have done that."

"Hey—you've done plenty of favors for me this trip. I think it's my turn to repay you. I'll bring the tray by in a few minutes."

"Merci, mon ami."

Gerard turned off his phone and finished listening.

"Who was that?"

"Mr. Smith. I'm afraid you're going to have to leave for a while. Under the circumstances, would you mind going to that shop we visited before and pick up the puppet I ordered for my daughter? Just in case I'm too sick to go anywhere tomorrow?"

The ploy had worked.

"You know I'd do anything for you."

"You're a treasure, Whitney. After your return, stay in your room. I'll phone you when the coast is clear and we'll spend the rest of the day and night together.

"Now, the money is in that manila envelope in my suitcase. The address is on the front. Just tell the taxi driver where you want to go and ask him to wait so he can bring you back. Here are some bills to pay the fare.''

"I won't be long.''

"Please hurry, Whitney.''

"I will. When we make love, Donald, I want you to speak French to me the whole time.''

Gerard shook his head in wonder. She'd said the perfect parting line to convince Bowen she was a starry-eyed teenager who didn't have a clue what was going on.

Two minutes later Gerard's cellular phone rang. That would be one of the agents in the surveillance van following her.

"Yes?''

"She's left the hotel.''

"Good. Stay right with her. Don't let anything happen to her.''

"She's important to you, this woman?''

His eyes closed tightly. "You have no idea.'' He clicked off.

Now it was *his* turn to go to work. Bowen was in for the surprise of his life! *This part was going to be fun.*

When Gerard thought about it, he hadn't had fun since the first moment he'd laid eyes on Whitney. Quite the reverse. Every minute had been a lesson in agony. Emotional, physical, mental and spiritual agony. *But that was about to end...*

"Ms. Lawrence?''

At the sound of her name being called out, she slowed her steps and turned in the direction of the male voice.

An attractive, dark-haired man stood just inside the door of the Salt Lake airline terminal where all the first-class passengers were deplaning the jet from Atlanta. He flashed her his credentials. *Roman Lufka, Private Investigator.*

Her heart began its galloping rhythm once more. "Are you a colleague of Hank's?" she cried out, desperate for news of him. "Is he all right? Please— I *have* to know." *Damn her tears.*

Her last day in Paris seemed to be part of some weird dream that had no basis in reality. One minute she'd been walking out of the puppet store with Donald Bowen's package. The next minute the police had rushed her to the airport in a van and had hustled her on board a 747 headed for the States.

There'd been no opportunity to say goodbye to Hank or to know if he was safe. The flight home had been pure torture for several reasons, not the least of which was this gut fear that she'd never see him again.

The light of compassion flared briefly in the other man's eyes. *Damn and damn again.* She'd revealed far too much of her feelings and could add embarrassment to the growing list of emotions which were tearing her apart.

"An hour ago I was informed by a reliable source that Mr. Smith is in New York taking a well-earned vacation."

"Thank heaven." Her voice shook.

The answer came as a mixed blessing. Knowing he was out of danger answered one of her prayers, the most important one, of course. That of being alive and unharmed. Still...

"Does he work here in Salt Lake? I—I'd like to thank him personally for all his help."

"I'm sure he would appreciate that, but I'm not at liberty to discuss any aspects of the case."

She swallowed hard. "Then could you tell me if he'll be coming to Salt Lake anytime soon?"

"I'm sorry. I wouldn't know his plans," the other man answered not unkindly. "I've been authorized to meet your plane and make sure you get home safely. Please come with me. I have your luggage."

"Thank you," she whispered.

The ride from the airport was accomplished in unnatural silence, but she felt too desolate to make conversation. It took all the willpower she could muster not to break down sobbing until after Mr. Lufka had driven her home and had thoroughly checked out her condo as a courtesy before saying goodbye.

Though Gerald had a drink in hand, and was comfortably ensconced in Yuri and Jeannie's study with two of his favorite people, he couldn't relax. The fear that Whitney had no romantic feelings for him had all but destroyed him.

Not at any time during those last two nights in his hotel room had she indicated that she desired him. *Hell.* They'd had all the time in the world to resume the intimacy they'd shared during the earlier part of the trip. But apparently it was all sham on her part. Once they'd flung away their masks, she'd wanted nothing more from him.

He was devastated.

He needed to hear from Roman that she was at least

home and safe. When the call came in on his cellular phone, he practically dropped his glass reaching for it.

"*Comrade?* Is that you? Did she get off that plane? Is she all right?"

The quiet coming from Roman's end began to sound more and more ominous. Gerard's body turned to ice. He lurched forward.

"*Roman?* What in the hell is wrong?"

At this point Jeannie and Yuri were on their feet, obviously alerted by the alarm in Gerard's voice.

He heard a heavy sigh coming from Roman's end. It had the impact of a blow to his midsection. "Tell me, dammit."

"*Comrade?*" Roman's grating voice was the worst of signs. "This is something I don't want to talk to you about over the phone. I think you'd better catch the next flight home. Let me know which one you're on. I'll meet your plane." The line went dead.

Jeannie rushed over and put an arm around his waist. "What's the matter? You're as white as a sheet."

"I don't know. I've never heard Roman sound like that before. Something tells me Whitney might have been hurt or possibly kidnapped in retaliation for my capturing Bowen." His voice broke. "I've got to go."

Yuri reached for his keys on the coffee table. "We'll drive you to the airport."

When the phone rang, Whitney had barely said good night to her family who had come over to her condo to welcome her home and hear about her trip to Mexico. Christine had been appreciative of the string puppet. The whole time they'd talked, she'd dangled it in front of Greg whose little fingers got all tangled in the strings. No one was the wiser.

As for Whitney, she was too heartbroken over her loss to worry about the lies she'd told them and reached numbly for the receiver.

"Hello?"

"Ms. Lawrence?"

Instantly alert, she thought she recognized the man's voice. Her heart started to hammer worse than before. "Mr. Lufka?"

"I shouldn't be giving you classified information, but you seemed so overwrought earlier, I thought you should know that Hank Smith will be arriving at the airport at eight-thirty p.m. tonight on Global Airlines' flight number 1240."

There was a disturbing pause. "I received a tip that he's not in the best shape. He may even require special care after he gets here. That's not the kind of news I like to give, but because you were directly involved in the case, I thought you deserved to know. Good night."

"*Wait—*" she cried out in panic, but he'd hung up.

She glanced at her watch. He'd be arriving within the hour. There was no time to lose. She *had* to get to the terminal ahead of him.

Thanks to Mr. Lufka, she would find a way to tell Hank how much she loved him before he was whisked off to some undisclosed location, possibly out of her sight forever.

Fortunately she'd been home since noon. Long enough to have showered and washed her hair. No longer needing to look eighteen, she wore it loose and flowing. The makeup helped her feel normal again.

Every time she happened to pass the mirror, she hardly recognized herself.

A quick search of her closet produced her favorite summer dress, an elegant outfit she hadn't taken on the tour. The thin black crepe with a muted gold print motif was a straight midcalf length and sleeveless. It tied at the back of her waist and could be dressed up or down with jewelry.

She chose to wear a chunky gold necklace above the modest neckline, and a matching bracelet with her watch. Her black leather sandals added the right touch. A dab of her favorite floral perfume and she was ready.

Tonight she needed to be sure she stood out in a crowd so Hank couldn't possibly miss her. No matter the state of his condition when he arrived, she wanted to look so beautiful for him he would never look anywhere else.

Alternating waves of fear and excitement held her in their grip as she drove her Jeep to the airport. The flight from New York would be crowded, which meant the terminal would be full of waiting loved ones as well as people anxious to board. Whitney intended to be at the head of the line, even if she had to bribe someone for space!

Before the jet had taxied to a stop, Gerard was out of his seat and ready to exit the first-class compartment. He'd tried repeatedly to reach Roman on the cellular phone, but there'd been no answer.

The flight had given him too much time to conjure various dangerous scenarios involving Whitney. Each one grew progressively more insupportable until he was sick to the pit of his stomach.

The second the passengers were allowed to disembark, he leaped into the opening ahead of the others and raced along the connecting walkway to the terminal.

As he ran into the lounge, a blur of black and gold entered his side vision. Because he was looking for Roman, it took a second for the vaguely familiar feminine image to register.

He slowed down and turned his head to make sure he wasn't hallucinating. That's when his feet came to a complete standstill.

Lord. It *was* Whitney. Tall, stunning. Gloriously alive.

She's headed your way, Roche. Those brilliant blues of hers are on fire for you.

"Hank—" She half-sobbed his name. Then she was running toward him, her arms outstretched.

His legs started to move again. He'd been living with so much pain, he could scarcely credit that this was really happening. But her warm arms were real, her luscious body was real. When he felt her melt into him, every doubt, every fear fled as if they had never existed.

"I love you," she repeated over and over again, burrowing against him in plain sight of the crowd. "I was so afraid something had happened to you and I would never be able to tell you. Mr. Lufka saw the state I was in and knew exactly how I felt. He said—"

"I know what he said," Gerard interrupted her, crushing her in his arms, burying his face in her gleaming, luxuriant hair. It was a long story. One day he'd tell Whitney all about the famous Lufkilovich brothers, the greatest con artists around. "He knew I was so in love with you, I needed to hear those words as soon as possible or my life wouldn't be worth living."

Unable to resist, he captured the mouth she willingly offered him. Words could no longer express the feelings erupting inside. Just like before, Whitney's kiss transformed him. He felt immortal.

From the beginning, love had been there on both their parts. His instincts hadn't been wrong. He'd never known this kind of happiness before. With the greatest of reluctance, he finally put her at arm's length. "How did you get here?"

"In my car," she answered breathlessly.

"Then let's go. I fell in love with an eighteen-year-old named Whitney Lawrence. Now I want to get to know Whitney Lawrence the woman. Together the two of you make the most beautiful sight this man has ever beheld."

Beyond the point of no return, they practically ran through the terminal to the parking area where they could be alone. Once inside the back seat of her Jeep, they reached for each other, unable to stand another second of separation.

For the next while she lost herself in his arms and clung feverishly to the mouth devouring hers. He was her heart's desire. She wanted nothing else. All the feelings and emotions they'd had to suppress throughout the tour came rushing to the forefront.

"You may think I'm moving things too fast, but I want to marry you as soon as we can arrange the ceremony. I'm so in love with you, Whitney, I can't even breathe anymore.''

"I feel the same way." Her voice shook. "I've wanted you for my husband longer than it's decent to admit, and I don't even know your last name."

"It's Roche," he said on a groan of deep satisfaction.

"Mrs. Eric-Gerard Roche. I love it. I love you," she cried, kissing him passionately once more. Wrapped in his arms, she didn't have to move a muscle to explore his features with her lips whenever she wanted. "Does everyone call you Eric-Gerard?"

He nodded. "Most people outside the agency. But Roman shortened it to Eric. Since then, it has been pared down to Gerard. Annabelle thought it was more romantic."

"Was she your wife?" Her heart pounded anxiously.

"No, darling. She's another PI with the agency. We had a few dates, nothing more. Now she's married to the man of her dreams.

"My wife, Simone, died in an avalanche in Switzerland in our twenties, but that was all a long time ago. Until I met you, I didn't think it was possible to feel this way about any woman again. You're my life, Whitney. I don't want to go on without you."

She clutched him tighter. "When I was put on the plane in Paris and thought I might never see you again, I wanted to die."

"You don't know how I've longed to hear those words. I was afraid there was someone else even though Roman hadn't uncovered a name."

"No one serious."

"That's hard to believe."

"Not really. My uncle is a psychiatrist and he told me I should take a lot of time and kiss a lot of frogs in several ponds until I met my prince. He was the most intelligent man I ever met, so I took his advice.

"On the flight to Europe you made me feel safe and cherished. You fit my image of the prince he'd been talking about. That's when my agony started, because I thought you were the man Christine had fallen in love with."

Gerard groaned. "My torture started when I saw this beautiful woman standing in line at the library. Even though she was young enough to be my daughter, my feelings were anything but fatherly."

She clung to him. "If I hadn't decided to track down my nephew's father, we would neve—"

He took a long time kissing her quiet. "I don't even want to think about it. One day I'll tell you the whole story about Bowen but for now let's just be grateful he's going to spend the rest of his life in prison where he belongs."

She nodded. "What excuse did you give the other teachers?"

"After the police made their arrest in his room, I got word to Mr. Grimshaw that Bowen had become acutely ill. Someone needed to accompany him to the hospital and stay with him.

"Grimshaw said he would pass the word to the others and make sure all the students, including Roger and Jeff, got back to Salt Lake safely. One day the news about Bowen will come out, of course. Until then, I could see no point in ruining everyone's trip.

"As for the disappearance of a certain Ms.

Lawrence, I told him you'd been worried about your grandmother and decided to take an early flight home.''

Whitney stared at him in awe. "You made a wonderful teacher, but you love being a PI, don't you?"

"How did you guess?"

"Because you're so good at it."

He smoothed the hair off her forehead. "After the performance you gave on the tour, I'm wondering if you're not in the wrong field. Roman would hire you in a shot."

"He must be a very good friend to do what he did for us tonight."

"He's like a brother."

"I thought so."

"You're going to love his brother Yuri, too."

"The man I met on the ferry in Geneva? He and Mr. Lufka look a lot alike."

Gerard nodded. "He and Jeannie live in New York."

"So *that's* where you were."

He smiled again. "They'll fly out for our wedding. The agency is like one happy family."

"It sounds wonderful."

"They'll all love you, but not as much as I do. Never as much as I do," he whispered rather emotionally. "Tomorrow I want to take you up the canyon to meet my parents. It's the one surprise they won't be expecting. They'll adore you."

"I can't wait to learn everything there is to know about you. Later on, we can stop by my parents' home. Christine and the baby live with them. Our news is going to make the family ecstatic. But there's just one thing—''

''What is it?''

''Since I've decided against telling Christine about Bowen, we're going to have to pretend we met in Mexico.''

''That's a good plan. We can work out the finer parts of our story later. Right now I just want to concentrate on us, but the back seat of your Jeep isn't exactly the place I had in mind.

''Much as I don't want to leave you for any reason, I need to pick up my bags and check in with Roman. Why don't you drive around in front of the terminal? I'll meet you there in a few minutes. Then we'll go wherever you want.''

''I just want to be with you. *Forever.*''

''That's fine, because I wasn't going to give you a choice.''

''Where's my little Greg? I have to hold him one more time before we leave.'' Whitney burst into Christine's bedroom and reached for her sleepy nephew who had been so perfect throughout the wedding ceremony and reception at her parents' home.

''I just fed him, so be careful. He might spit up on your beautiful new suit,'' Christine cried. ''That rose silk is beautiful on you. Here, let me at least put a clean cloth on your shoulder.''

Whitney thanked her sister and held the baby close. He was almost seven months now and growing more adorable every day.

Much as Whitney despised what Donald Bowen had done, she was crazy about Greg and couldn't imagine